C.J.S. Thompson

Poison Romance and Poison Mysteries

Outlook

C.J.S. Thompson

Poison Romance and Poison Mysteries

1. Auflage | ISBN: 978-3-73262-940-4

Erscheinungsort: Frankfurt am Main, Deutschland

Erscheinungsjahr: 2018

Outlook Verlag GmbH, Frankfurt.

IN THE NECESSARY TOIL

AND

SUFFERING OF THIS LIFE

MAN CAN INVENT NOTHING NOBLER THAN HUMANITY!

THEN WHAT HIGHER AIM CAN MAN ATTAIN THAN CONQUEST OVER HUMAN PAIN?

ENO'S 'FRUIT SALT' prevents unnecessary suffering and removes disease only by natural laws.

READ the 20-page pamphlet given with each bottle!

ENO'S 'FRUIT SALT' rectifies the Stomach, and makes the Liver laugh with joy by natural means (Or, in other words, Gentleness does more than Violence.)

1

Its universal success proves the truth of the above assertion.

MORAL FOR ALL—

"I need not be missed if another succeed me;

To reap down those fields which in spring I have sown.

He who ploughed and who sowed is not missed by the reaper,

He is only remembered by what he has done."

The effect of Eno's 'Fruit Salt' upon any Disordered and Feverish Condition is Simply Marvellous. It is, in fact, Nature's Own Remedy, and is an Unsurpassed One.

CAUTION.—*Examine the Capsule, and see that it is marked ENO'S 'FRUIT SALT,' otherwise you have the sincerest form of flattery— IMITATION.*

Prepared only by J. C. ENO, Ltd., 'FRUIT SALT' WORKS, LONDON, S.E., by J. C. ENO'S Patent.

POISON ROMANCE AND POISON MYSTERIES

POISON ROMANCE AND
POISON MYSTERIES

BY

C. J. S. THOMPSON.

St. James' Gazette:—"There is indeed no more fascinating reading … very pleasant and readable…. It is full of good reading, with some rather creepy and *saugrenu* dippings into the past."

Daily Chronicle:—"Poison is always a fascinating subject. There is something subtle and mystic about the very word. On this attractive theme Mr. THOMPSON has collected a great deal of information from ancient and modern alike."

Daily Mail:—"People who are fond of prying into the gruesome subject of toxicology will find some interesting chapters in Mr. C. J. S. THOMPSON's book."

The Athenæum:—"Decidedly sensible and well informed."

Literature:—"Mr. THOMPSON writes a sprightly chapter on toxicology in fiction."

The Saturday Review:—"A great deal of curious information concerning the history of poisons and poisonings."

Illustrated London News:—"The story portions will attract most attention, and the poisoned gloves and rings of old romance supply satisfaction to that sensational instinct which is absent in hardly one of us."

The Queen:—"Will fascinate most people. Is very readably written. Its only fault is that it is too short."

Liverpool Courier:—"It is a readable book as well as an able one. The author is an eminent toxicologist and writes pleasantly on the lore connected with the science."

The Scotsman:—"It is successful and interesting. Full of odd and startling information."

Manchester Courier:—"The book is extremely interesting and particularly valuable."

Aberdeen Free Press:—"Fascinates the majority of his readers. One could wish that Mr. THOMPSON had written much more."

Glasgow Citizen:—"A book of the week."

Glasgow Herald:—"Light and eminently readable."

_ An edition of this book in cloth boards, price 2*s.* 6*d.*, is published by The Scientific Press Ltd., 28 & 29, Southampton Street, Strand, London, W.C.

POISON ROMANCE AND POISON MYSTERIES

BY

C. J. S. THOMPSON, F.R.Hist.S.

AUTHOR OF "THE MYSTERY AND ROMANCE OF ALCHEMY AND PHARMACY" "THE
CHEMIST'S COMPENDIUM" "A MANUAL OF PERSONAL HYGIENE" "PHARMACY AND
DISPENSING" ETC. ETC.

LONDON

GEORGE ROUTLEDGE & SONS, LTD

BROADWAY HOUSE, LUDGATE HILL, E.C.

1904

ROUTLEDGE'S
CAXTON
LIBRARY

OF

Fiction and Standard Works

Medium 8vo.   Price **6d.** *each.*

OVER 300 VOLUMES.

PREFACE TO FIRST EDITION

Iɴ response to the wishes of many who read this work when it appeared in serial form, it is now reproduced with much additional matter, which I hope may prove of value to those interested in the fascinating subject of poisons and the study of toxicology. It has been my endeavour to collect, in the following pages, the scattered fragments of historic and romantic lore connected with poisons from the earliest period, and to recount the stories of some notable "poison mysteries" of ancient and modern times. I am indebted to the works of Dr. Wynter Blyth for many facts concerning the poisons of antiquity.

C. J. S. T.

1899

PREFACE TO NEW EDITION

Iɴ presenting a new edition of this work to my readers, the opportunity has been taken to introduce several new chapters, one of which deals with the "poison mystery" which recently aroused such widespread interest in the United States. In response to suggestions, detailed accounts of the "Horsford case" and the "Lambeth poison mysteries" have also been added.

C. J. S. T.

CONTENTS

POISON ROMANCE AND POISON MYSTERIES

CHAPTER I

L<small>ONG</small> before the action of vegetable and mineral substances on human beings and animals was known, it is probable that poisonous bodies in some form were used by primitive man.

When injured in battle by perhaps a flint arrow-head, or stone axe, he sought for something to revenge himself on his enemy. In his search after curative remedies he also found noxious ones, which produced unpleasant effects when applied to the point of a weapon destined to enter the internal economy of an opponent.

He doubtless also became aware that the spear-points and arrow-heads on which the blood of former victims had dried, caused wounds that rapidly proved fatal, owing to the action of what we now call septic poisons. This probably led to experiments with the juices of plants, until something of a more deadly character was discovered.

This was the very earliest age of poisoning, when pharmacy was employed for vicious or revengeful purposes.

Thus we find that almost every savage nation and people has its own peculiar poison. In Africa the seeds of *Strophanthus hispidus*, or kombé, a most virulent poison, are used for this purpose; while explorers tell us that the ancient pigmy race of Central Africa employ a species of red ant crushed to a paste, to tip their arrows and spears. The South American Indians poison their arrow-heads with curare or ourari, produced from a species of *strychnos* and other plants, while the Malays and hill tribes of India use aconite, and other poisonous juices and extracts. The *Antiaris toxicaria* is also used as an arrow poison by the Malays.

The bushmen of the South African district "Kalahari," use the juice of the leaf beetle "diamphidia" and its larva for poisoning their arrow-heads. Lewin, who calls the beetle *Diamphidia simplex*, found in its body, besides inert fatty acids, a toxalbumin which causes paralysis, and finally death. According to Boehm, the poison from the larva also belongs to the toxalbumins, and Starke states, that it causes the dissolution of the colouring matter of the blood and produces inflammation.

A halo of mystery, sometimes intermixed with romance, has hung about the dread word *poison* from very early times. In the dark days of mythology, allusions to mysterious poisons were made in legend and saga. Thus a country in the Far North was supposed to be ruled and dominated by sorcerers and kindred beings, all of whom were said to be children of the Sun. Here dwelt Æëtes, Perses, Hecate, Medea, and Circe. Hecate was the daughter of Perses and married to Æëtes, and their daughters were Medea and Circe. Æëtes and Perses were said to be brothers, and their country was afterwards supposed to be Colchis. To Hecate is ascribed the foundation of sorcery and the discovery of poisonous herbs. Her knowledge of magic and spells was supposed to be unequalled. She transmitted her power to Medea, whose wonderful exploits have been frequently described and depicted, and who by her magic arts subdued the dragon that guarded the golden fleece, and assisted Jason to perform his famous deeds. Hecate's garden is described by the poets as being enclosed in lofty walls with thrice-folding doors of ebony, which were guarded by terrible forms, and only those who bore the leavened rod of expiation and the concealed conciliatory offering could enter. Towering above was the temple of the dread sorceress, where the ghastly sacrifices were offered and all kinds of horrible spells worked.

Medea was also learned in sorcery and an accomplished magician. It is related that, after her adventures with Jason, she returned with him to Thessaly. On their arrival they found Æson, the father of Jason, and Pelias, his uncle, who had usurped the throne, both old and decrepit. Medea was requested to exert her magical powers to make the old man young again, an operation she is said to have speedily performed by infusing the juice of certain potent plants into his veins.

Some years after, Medea deserted Jason and fled to Athens, and shortly afterwards married Ægeus, king of that city. Ægeus had a son by a former wife, named Theseus, who had been brought up in exile. At length he resolved to return and claim his parentage, but Medea hearing of this, and for some reason greatly resenting it, put a poisoned goblet into the hands of Ægeus at an entertainment he gave to Theseus, with the intent that he should hand it to his son. At the critical moment, however, the king cast his eyes on the sword of Theseus, and at once recognized it as that which he had delivered to his son when a child, and had directed that it should be brought by him when a man, as a token of the mystery of his birth. The goblet was at once thrown away, the father embraced his son, and Medea fled from Athens in a chariot drawn by dragons through the air.

Circe's charms were of a more seductive and romantic character. She is said to have been endowed with exquisite beauty, which she employed to allure travellers to her territory. On their landing, she entreated and enticed them to drink from her enchanted cup. But no sooner was the draught swallowed, than the unfortunate stranger was turned into a hog, and driven by the magician to her sty, where he still retained the consciousness of what he had been, and lived to repent his folly.

Gula, the patroness of medicine and a divinity of the Accadians, was regarded by that ancient people as "the mistress and controller of noxious poisons" as far back as 5000 years B.C.

According to some authorities, the Hebrew word *Chasaph*, translated in the Old Testament Scriptures as witch, meant poisoner. Scott states the witches of Scripture had probably some resemblance to those of ancient Europe, who, although their skill and power might be safely despised as long as they confined themselves to their charms and spells, were very apt to eke out their capacity for mischief by the use of actual poison; so that the epithet of sorceress and poisoner were almost synonymous.

The oldest Egyptian king, Menes, and Attalus Phylometer, the last king of Pergamus, were both learned in the knowledge of the properties of plants. The latter monarch also knew something of their medicinal uses, and was acquainted with henbane, aconite, hemlock, hellebore, etc. Other Egyptian rulers cultivated the art of medicine, and there is little doubt that, probably through the priests, who were the chief practitioners of the art of healing, they gathered a considerable knowledge of the properties of many poisonous and other herbs. Prussic acid was known to the Egyptians, and prepared by them in a diluted form, from the peach and other plants. It is highly probable, indeed, that the priests had some rudimentary knowledge of the process of distillation, and prepared this deadly liquid from peach leaves or stones, by that method. The "penalty of the peach" is alluded to in a papyrus now preserved in the Louvre, which points to the liquid being used as a death draught.

The ancient Greeks, like the Chinese of to-day, looked upon suicide, under certain conditions, as a noble act, for which poison was the usual medium. Their "death cup" was mainly composed of the juice or extract of a species of hemlock, called by them cicuta. The Chinese, from remote times, are supposed to have used gold as a poison, especially for suicidal purposes, and at the present day, when a high official or other individual puts an end to his life, it is always officially announced, "He has taken gold leaf"; a curious phrase, which probably has its origin in antiquity.

Nicander, of Colophon, a Greek physician, who lived 204-138 B.C., in his work on "Poisons and their Antidotes," the earliest on the subject known, describes the effects of snake venom and the properties of opium, henbane, colchicum, cantharides, hemlock, aconite, toxicum (probably the venom of the toad), buprestis, the salamander, the sea-hare, the leech, yew (decomposed), bull's blood, milk, and certain fungi, which he terms "evil fermentations of the earth"; and as antidotes for the same he mentions lukewarm oil, warm water, and mallow or linseed tea to excite vomiting. The same writer also made a rough classification of the poisons known in his time, twenty-two in all, and divided them into two classes—viz., "those which killed quickly," and "those which killed slowly."

Of the minerals, arsenic, antimony, mercury, gold, silver, copper, and lead were used by the Greeks; the antidote recommended in case of poisoning being hot oil, and other methods to induce vomiting and prevent the poison being absorbed into the system.

Bull's blood is classed as a poison by various ancient writers, and it is recorded that Æson, Midas King of Phrygia, Plutarch, and Themistocles, killed themselves by drinking bull's blood. It is probable that some strong poisonous vegetable substance, such as cicuta, was mixed with the blood.

Dioscorides throws a further light on the poisons of antiquity in his great work on Materia Medica, which for fifteen centuries or more remained the chief authority on that subject. He mentions cantharides, copper, mercury, lead, and arsenic. Among the animal poisons are included toads, salamanders, poisonous snakes, a peculiar kind of honey, and the blood of the ox, probably after it had turned putrid. The sea-hare is frequently alluded to by the ancient Greeks, and was evidently regarded by them as capable of producing a very powerful poison. Domitian is said to have administered it to Titus. It is supposed to have been one of the genus *Aplysia*, among the gasteropods, and is described by the old writers as a dreadful object, which was neither to be touched nor looked upon with safety.

Among the poisonous plants enumerated by Dioscorides are the poppy, black and white hellebore, henbane, mandragora, hemlock, elaterin, and the juices of species of euphorbia, and apocyneæ. Medea is said to have been the first to introduce colchicum. The black and white hellebore were known to the Romans, and used by them as an insecticide, and Pliny states that the Gauls used a preparation of veratrum to poison their arrows. Arsenic was employed by the Greeks as a caustic, and for removing hair from the face; while copper, mercury, and lead were used in their medical treatment. The study of poisons was forbidden for a long period, and Galen mentions the fact that only a few philosophers dared treat the subjects in their works.

In the East, poisons have been used from remote times, not only for the destruction of human life, but also for destroying animals—arsenic, aconite, and opium being employed by the Asiatics for these purposes. The Hindoos have many strange traditions concerning poisons, some being attributed with the property of causing a lingering death, which can be controlled by the will of the poisoner. But this is doubtless more legendary than correct. One curious and mysterious substance mentioned by Blyth, and known in India as *Mucor phycomyces*, is stated to be a species of fungi. When the spores are administered in warm water they are said to attach themselves to the throat and rapidly develop and grow, with the result that in a few weeks, all the symptoms of consumption develop, and the victim is rapidly carried off by that fatal disease.

The early Hebrews were also acquainted with certain poisons, the words, "rosch" and "chema" being used by them as generic terms. Arsenic was known to them as "sam," aconite as "boschka," and ergot probably as "son."

The ancients attributed poisonous properties to certain bodies simply on account of their origin being mysterious and obscure, and many of these errors and traditions have been handed down for centuries. As an instance of this, the belief that diamond dust possessed deadly poisonous properties seems to have existed until recent times. Many mysterious deaths in the Middle Ages were attributed to it. There is little doubt that death might be caused by the mere mechanical effect of an insoluble powder of this kind, if it were possible to introduce it into the stomach in sufficient quantity, but powdered glass or sand would have the same effect as diamond dust, viz. in causing violent irritation of the stomach. Yet some of these old traditions have a substratum of fact.

The poisonous properties of the toad have long been regarded as fabulous, but recent investigation has proved that the skin of a species of toad secretes a poison, similar in action to digitalis.

The venom of the toad has had the reputation of possessing poisonous properties from a very early period, and was probably one of the earliest forms of animal poison known.

The old tradition, that King John was poisoned by a Friar who dropped a toad into his wine, was regarded as a ridiculous fable until some years ago, when it was discovered that the skin of the toad secretes a body, the active principle of which, "phrynin," is a poison of considerable power.

One of the most curious uses to which the toad has been put is recorded on a medical diploma now in the Library of Ferrara, which was granted to one Generoso Marini in 1642. Marini having made application for a Ferrarese diploma in medicine, the judges in whom the power of granting such degrees was invested, ordered him to exhibit some efficient proofs of his capability to practise the medical art.

Marini at once agreed to comply with their demand, and the result is recorded in his diploma, which was discovered by Cittadella in the archives of Ferrara, and is translated as follows:—

"Having publicly examined and approved the science and knowledge of medicine of Signor Generoso Marini, and his possession of the wonderful secret called 'Orvietano,' which he exhibited on the stage built in the centre of this our city of Ferrara, in presence of its entire population so remarkable for their civilization and learning, and in presence of many foreigners and other classes of people, we hereby certify that, also in our presence, as well as that of the city authorities, he took several living toads, not those of his own providing, but from a great number of toads which had been caught in fields in the locality by persons who were strangers to him, and which were only handed to him at the moment of making the experiment. An officer of the court then selected from the number of toads collected, five of the largest, which the said Generoso Marini placed on a bench before him, and in presence of all assembled spectators, he, with a large knife, cut all the said toads in half. Then, taking a drinking cup, he took in each hand one half of a dead toad, and squeezed from it all the juices and fluids it contained into the cup, and the same he did with the remainder. After mixing the contents together, he swallowed the whole, and then placing the cup on the bench he advanced to the edge of the stage, where for some minutes he remained stationary. Then he became pale as death and his limbs trembled, and his body began to swell in a frightful and terrible manner; and all the spectators began to believe that he would never recover from the poison he had swallowed, and that his death was certain. Suddenly, taking from a jar by his side some of his celebrated 'Orvietano,' he placed a portion of it in his mouth and swallowed it. Instantly, the effect of this wonderful medicine was to make him vomit the poison he had taken, and he stood before the spectators in the full enjoyment of health.[1]

"The populace applauded him highly for the indisputable proof he had given of his talent, and he then invited many of the most learned of those present to accompany him to his house, and he there showed them his dispensary as well as his collection of antidotes, and among them a powder made from little vipers, a powerful remedy for curing every sort of fever, as he had proved by different experiments he had made on people of quality and virtue, all of whom he had cured of the fever from which they were suffering, etc.

"In consequence of the rare talent exhibited by Signor Generoso Marini, and as a proof of our love and respect for his wisdom, we have resolved by the authority placed in our hands publicly to reward him with a diploma, so that he may be universally recognized, applauded, and respected. In witness thereof we have set our hands and the public seal of the municipality of Ferrara.

"Data in Ferrara con grandissimo applauso il di 26 Luglio, 1642.

"JOANNES CAJETANUS MODONI,
  "*Index sapientum Civitatis Ferrari.*

"FRANCISCUS ALTRAMARI,
  "*Cancellarius.*"

But although the toad under certain conditions was credited with poisonous properties, during the Middle Ages it was esteemed a valuable remedy for the plague, and was employed for that purpose in Austria as late as the year 1712.

Cantharides, or Spanish fly, was very commonly used as a poison in mediæval times, the usual method of administering being to chop it up and mix it with pepper. It is said to have been the first poison tried on the unfortunate Sir Thomas Overbury, although his murderers finally finished him off with corrosive sublimate. Poisoned rings are said to have been the invention of the Italians, who fashioned rings in which the poison was inserted in a receptacle where the jewel is usually set. Attached to the inner part of the ring was a sharp point which, when the hand of the wearer was grasped, scratched the flesh and injected the poison. Rings were also used for carrying strong poisons secretly—such as arsenic, or corrosive sublimate— and in this manner many were enabled to commit suicide after being imprisoned.

Hyoscyamus, commonly called henbane, is a herb which has been employed from remote times. Benedictus Crispus, Archbishop of Milan, in a work written shortly before A.D. 681, alludes to it under the name of hyoscyamus and symphoniaca, and in the tenth century its virtues are particularly recorded by Macer Floridus. In the early Anglo-Saxon works it is called henbell and sometimes belene. In a French herbal of the fifteenth century it is called hanibane or hanebane. From a very early period it has been employed as a sedative and anodyne, for producing sleep, although simple hallucinations sometimes accompany its use.

An old tradition states, that once in the refectory of an ancient monastery the monks were served with henbane, instead of some harmless root, in error by the cook. After partaking of the dish, they were seized with the most extraordinary hallucinations. At midnight one monk sounded the bell for matins, while others walked in the chapel and opened their books, but could not read. Others sang roystering drinking songs and performed mountebank antics, which convulsed the others with uncontrollable laughter, and the pious monastery for the nonce was turned into an asylum. Certain stones which were sold for large sums of money were supposed to change colour when brought near a poisonous substance, and they were consequently much sought after by high personages. The horn of the unicorn was said to become moist when placed near poisoned food. Bickman records his belief that several slow poisons were known to the ancients which cannot now be identified. The Carthaginians also seem to have been acquainted with similar poisons, and, according to tradition, administered some to Regulus, the Roman general. But we cannot endorse Bickman's belief.

An incident which happened to the army led by Mark Antony against the Parthians, and described by Plutarch, is said to have been caused by aconite. At one time during the expedition, "the soldiers being very short of provisions, sought for roots and pot-herbs ... and met one that brought on madness and death. The eater immediately lost all memory and knowledge, busying himself at the same time in turning and moving every stone he met with, as if he were on some important pursuit. The camp was full of unhappy men stooping to the ground, and digging up and removing stones, till at last they were carried off by bilious vomiting.... Whole numbers perished, and the Parthians still continued to harass them. Antony is said to have frequently exclaimed: 'Oh! the ten thousand!' alluding to the army which Xenophon led in retreat; both a longer way and through more numerous conflicts, and yet led in safety."

Nine active or virulent poisons are mentioned by most ancient writers on Indian medicine, many of which are at present not identified. Most of them are apparently varieties of aconite. Besides these, they employed opium, gunja, datura, roots of *Nerium odorum* and *Gloriosa superba*, the milky juices of *Calotropis gigantea* and *Euphorbia neriifolia*, white arsenic, orpiment, and the poison extracted from the fangs of serpents.

Most of the older Sanscrit MSS. are written on paper prepared with orpiment to preserve them from the ravages of insects. Three varieties of *Datura* yield atropine, a powerful poison. These plants were frequently employed in India for putting a sudden end to domestic quarrels, and to this practice may be traced the origin of the custom of "Suttee," or widow burning, as the Brahmins found from experience that, by making a wife's life conterminous with the husband's the average husband lived considerably longer.

It is worthy of note that the diamond was celebrated as a medicinal agent by the Hindoos, who prepared it by roasting seven times and then reducing it to powder. It was given in doses of one grain as a powerful tonic.

[1] The celebrated "Orvietano" was doubtless some preparation of antimony.

CHAPTER II

AMONG the ignorant, poisons have ever been closely associated with superstition, and thus we find in the dark ages, even among the more civilized nations of the West, a belief in the occult concerning those things the action of which they did not understand. To most of the poisonous herbs used by the ancients certain curious superstitions were attached. The mandrake, in particular, excited the greatest veneration on this account. It is supposed this plant is the same which the ancient Hebrews called Dudaïm. That these people held it in the highest esteem in the days of Jacob is evident from the notice of its having been found by Reuben, who carried it to his mother; and the inducement which tempted Leah to part with it proves the value then set upon this remarkable plant. It was believed to possess the property of making childless wives become mothers. Mandrake was among the more important drugs employed by the ancients for producing anæsthesia. Doses of the wine made from the root were administered before amputating a limb or the application of the hot iron cautery. Pliny says: "Mandrake is taken against serpents, and before cutting and puncture, lest they be felt. Sometimes the smell is sufficient." According to Apuleius, half an ounce of the wine would make a person insensible even to the pain of amputation. Lyman states it was this wine, "mingled with myrrh," that was offered to the Saviour on the Cross, it being commonly given to those who suffered death by crucifixion to allay in some degree their terrible agonies. In Shakespeare's time mandrake still kept its place in public estimation as a narcotic. Thus we have Cleopatra asking for the drug, that she may "sleep out this great gap of time" while her Antony is away; and Iago, when his poison begins to work in the mind of the Moor, exclaims—

"Not poppy, nor mandragora

Nor all the drowsy syrups of this world, Shal‏.

ever medicine thee to that sweet sleep."

Some of the old names applied to the plant, such as semihomo and anthropomorphon, refer to the appearance of the root, while the term "love-apples" applied to the fruit relates to their imaginary aphrodisiacal properties. It is mentioned in the Scriptures in connexion with such episodes. Josephus states "baaras" (supposed to be mandrake) was capable of expelling demons from those possessed. Demosthenes, the Athenian orator, is said to have compared his lethargic hearers to those who had eaten mandrake. Dioscorides states that "a drachm of mandragora taken in a draught, or eaten in a cake, causes infatuation, and takes away the use of reason." The Greeks bestowed on it the name of "Circeium" derived from the witch Circe. They believed that when the mandrake was dragged up from the earth, it gave a dreadful shriek, and struck the daring person dead who had had the presumption to pull it up. The method of obtaining it, therefore, was by fastening the plant to the tail of a dog, who thus drew the root from the ground. The shriek was supposed to be due to an evil spirit who dwelt in the plant. The Romans also were very particular in the manner in which they obtained the root. Pliny tells us that he who would undertake this office should stand with his back to the wind, and before he begins to dig, make three circles round the plant with the point of a sword, and then turning to the west proceed to take it up. The small roots, which are much twisted and gnarled, sometimes bear a resemblance to the form of man, and this was turned to account by some of the old German doctors, who fashioned them into rude images and sold them as preventives of evil and danger. They called them Abrunes. These images were regularly dressed every day and consulted as oracles and were manufactured in great numbers. They were introduced into England in the time of Henry VIII, and met with ready purchasers. To increase their value and importance, the roots were said by the vendors to be produced from the flesh of criminals which fell from the gibbet and that they only grew in such situations. Lord Bacon notices their use in the following paragraph—"Some plants there are, but rare, that have a morsie or downie root, and likewise that have a number of threads like beards, as mandrakes, whereof witches and impostours make an ugly image, giving it the form of a face at the top of the root, and these strings to make a broad beard down to the foot." Madame de Genlis states that "the mandrake roots should be wrapped in a sheet, for that then they will bring increasing good luck." The plant is still used medicinally in China, where it is said to be largely taken by the mandarins, who believe it will give them increased intellectual powers and prolong their lives. From recent investigation the activity of the mandrake root is proved to be due to an alkaloid called mandragorine.

The black hellebore, Melampus root or Christmas rose, another poisonous plant known to the ancients, was believed to have magical properties. It was called after Melampus, a great physician, who flourished at Pylos, about one hundred years after the time of Moses, or about one thousand five hundred and thirty years before the birth of Christ. He is reputed to have cured the daughters of Prœtus, King of Argos, of mental derangement with hellebore. Pliny mentions that the daughters of Prœtus were restored to their senses by drinking the milk of goats which had fed on hellebore. Black hellebore root was used by the ancients to purify their homes and to hallow their dwellings, and they believed that by strewing it about it would drive away evil spirits. This ceremony was performed with great devotion, and accompanied with the singing of solemn hymns. They also blessed their cattle in the same manner with hellebore to keep them free from spells of the wicked. For these purposes it was dug up with many religious ceremonies—such as drawing a circle round the plant with a sword; then, turning to the east, a humble prayer was finally offered up by the devotee, to Apollo and Aesculapius for leave to dig up the root. The flight of the eagle was particularly attended to during the ceremony, for when this bird approached near the spot during the celebration of the rite, it was considered so ominous as to predict the certain death of the person who uprooted the plant in the course of the year. Others ate garlic previous to the rite, which was supposed to counteract the poisonous effluvia of the plant. Dioscorides relates that when Carneades, the Cyrenaic philosopher, undertook to answer the books of Zeno, he sharpened his wit and quickened his spirit by purging his head with powdered hellebore. It is recorded that the Gauls never went to the chase without rubbing the point of their arrows with this herb, believing that it rendered all the game killed with them the more tender. It is of this plant Juvenal sarcastically observes: "Misers need a double dose of hellebore."

With several uncivilised nations in Africa, the practice of compelling persons accused of crime or witchcraft to undergo the ordeal of swallowing some vegetable poison is still carried on. For this purpose certain tribes in Western Africa use the Calabar bean, sometimes called the ordeal bean, which contains a powerful poisonous principle, called Physostigmine. It was customary, at one time, in Old Calabar, and the mouth of the Niger, where the plant grows, to destroy it whenever found, a few only being preserved to supply seeds for judicial purposes, and of these seeds the store was kept in the custody of the native chief. Witchcraft, indeed, may be said to play the chief part in the daily life of all African natives, and to witchcraft they attribute every ill that befalls them. Two classes of witchcraft are supposed to exist— the one practised secretly by evil-doers, and the other practised by the witch doctors with the view of destroying the effects of the former. Witch doctors are, in fact, the greatest power in the land; they hold the lives of all in their hands, and are daily employed to satisfy the passions of their neighbours. "According to native ideas," says one who has had a long experience among the native tribes, "death or sickness never occurs through natural causes, but is always the result of somebody's act. Whenever any one is accused of having practised witchcraft, or of having committed any other crime, Calabar bean or Muavi is used to decided the case. The taking of these is the great trial by ordeal, and, usually, except when the accuser is a witch doctor, accused and accuser have both to submit to the test. Chiefs, however, may appoint a deputy to undergo the ordeal in their stead. Muavi consists of a specially prepared drug, usually made by scraping the wood of a certain tree known to the witch doctors; this is mixed with water, and both parties swallow the decoction. In a very short time the drug begins to act. Vomiting sets in, followed by convulsions and death. Of course, in most cases the result depends on the dose given. Sometimes both accuser and accused are seized with vomiting; in that case the natives say that the medicine has been badly prepared, and the operation is repeated. At other times both die; in that case also the medicine was no good, but the trial cannot be renewed, as may be readily understood. When the guilt of one of the parties has been established by his death, his property is at once looted, his wife and children being killed. So great, however, is the faith of the natives in the infallibility of the Muavi test, and they so fully believe that in case of innocence they will be proof against the deadly effects of the drug, that they will never hesitate to submit themselves to the trial; in fact, they will frequently volunteer to go through it, and insist upon taking muavi even when falsely accused. From this account it will be easily seen that the witch doctor who prepares the muavi can easily get rid of any person he may wish. In some districts the drug used for the trial, instead of causing death, when it has not acted as an emetic, merely causes purging; but the result is the same, as the man is at once put to death." This is probably due to a weaker decoction of the drug having been prepared. The same traveller states, in many instances his own men have offered to take muavi in order to refute the slightest charge. Trial by ordeal, which still survives in the Dark Continent, was practised by other and more civilized nations in the early Christian era.

CHAPTER III

ROYAL AND HISTORIC POISONERS

POISON appears to have been employed as a political agent from a very early period of history, and numerous stories have been handed down of royal personages who used this secret and deadly method of ridding themselves of troublesome individuals, and removing enemies from their path. They also, at times, became the victims of jealous rivals by the same nefarious means.

One of the earliest traditions we have of this kind is that of Phrysa, who poisoned the queen Statira during the reign of Artaxerxes II (Mnemon), B.C. 405-359, by cutting her food with a poisoned knife. The notorious Nero doubtless resorted to the use of poison more than once, as may be inferred from the story of the death of his brother Britannicus, who, it is said, was poisoned by his orders. Britannicus was dining with his brother and the Imperial family, and, as was the custom of the Romans, hot water was brought round by slaves to the table, the water being heated to varied degrees to suit the taste of the drinker. According to the story, the cup of water handed to Britannicus proved to be too hot, and he gave it back to the attendant slave, who added cold water to it, which addition is supposed to have contained the poison; for no sooner had he swallowed the draught than he fell back gasping for breath. His mother, Agrippina, and Octavia, his sister, who were also at the table, became terror-stricken, but Nero, unmoved, calmly remarked that he often had such fits in his youth without danger, and the banquet proceeded. It is thought probable that the poison given was prussic acid in some form.

A curious superstition existed in early times, and is still entertained by the ignorant, that if the body rapidly decomposes after a sudden death it is to be attributed to the effects of poison. So when Britannicus died, it is recorded that the Romans attempted to conceal his discoloured face by means of paint. During the Roman period, poisoning was reduced to a fine art, and the skilled or professional poisoner obtained large amounts of money for his services.

The Borgias' favourite method of administering a lethal dose was by means of a species of hypodermic injection.

The greatest craft and cunning used to be exerted in order to introduce poison into the system, and there are many old traditions concerning the subtle methods employed, although a number of these are doubtless more legendary than correct. Thus Tissot states that John, King of Castile, owed his death to wearing a pair of boots which were supposed to have been impregnated with poison by a Turk. Henry VI is said to have succumbed through wearing poisoned gloves and Louis XIV and Pope Clement VII through the fumes from a poisoned taper. King John is supposed to have been poisoned by matter extracted from a living toad placed in his wassail bowl, while Pope Alexander VI is said also to have fallen a victim to poison, "after which," according to the chronicler, "his body presented a fearful spectacle."

A document drawn up by Charles, King of Navarre, throws some light on the systematic manner in which the poisoning of obnoxious persons was carried out in mediæval times. It is in the form of a commission to one Wondreton to poison Charles VI, the Duke of Valois, brother of the King, and his uncles, the Dukes of Berri, Burgundy, and Bourbon. It runs: "Go thou to Paris; thou canst do great service if thou wilt. Do what I tell thee; I will reward thee well. There is a thing which is called sublimed arsenic; if a man eat a bit the size of a pea, he will never survive. Thou wilt find it in Pampeluna, Bordeaux, Bayonne, and in all the good towns thou wilt pass at the apothecaries' shops. Take it, and powder it; and when thou shalt be in the house of the King, of the Count de Valois his brother, and the Dukes of Berri, Burgundy, and Bourbon, draw near and betake thyself to the kitchen, to the larder, to the cellar, or any other place where thy point can best be gained, and put the powder in the soups, meats, or wines; provided that thou canst do it secretly. Otherwise do it not." It is satisfactory to learn that the miscreant who was intrusted with this diabolical commission, was detected in time, and executed in 1384.

It is related of Charles IX that, having suspected one of his cooks of stealing two silver spoons, he resolved to try the effect of bezoar, which at that time was highly recommended as an antidote to poisons. So, thinking a good opportunity had arrived for testing its properties, his Majesty administered to the unfortunate cook, first, a large dose of corrosive sublimate, and then a dose of the reputed antidote; but the unlucky man fell a victim to the experiment, and died in great agony in seven hours, in spite of other efforts to save him.

There is an old tradition that King John also figured as a poisoner, and got rid of the unfortunate Maud Fitz-Walter by means of a poisoned egg. The story is a romantic one, and is related by Hepworth Dixon in "Her Majesty's Tower." "In the reign of King John, the White Tower received one of the first and fairest of a long line of female victims, in that of Maud Fitz-Walter, who was known to the singers of her time as Maud the Fair. The father of this beautiful girl was Robert, Lord Fitz-Walter, of Castle Baynard, on the Thames, one of John's most powerful and greatest barons. Yet the King, during, it is said, a fit of violence or temper with the Queen, fell madly in love with the fair Maud. As neither the lady herself nor her powerful sire would listen to his disgraceful suit, the King is said to have seized her by force at Dunmow and brought her to the Tower. Fitz-Walter raised an outcry, on which the King sent troops into Castle Baynard and his other houses, and when the baron protested against these wrongs, his master banished him from the realm. Fitz-Walter fled to France with his wife and other children, leaving poor Maud in the Tower, where she suffered a daily insult in the King's unlawful suit. But she remained obdurate, and refused his offers. On her proud and scornful answer to his overtures being heard, John carried her up to the roof and locked her in the round turret, standing on the north-east angle of the keep. Maud's cage was the highest and chilliest den in the Tower; but neither cold, solitude, nor hunger could break her strength, and at last, in the rage of his disappointed love, the King sent one of his minions to her room with a poisoned egg, of which the brave girl ate and died."

Bluff King Hal at one period of his life was apprehensive of being poisoned, and it was commonly believed that Anne Boleyn attempted to dose him. It is recorded that the King, in an interview with young Prince Henry, burst into tears, saying that he and his sister, the Princess Mary, might thank God for having escaped from the hands of that accursed and venomous harlot, who had intended to poison them.

According to the French Chronicles, "After the death of Gaultier Giffard, Count Buckingham, in the early part of the twelfth century, Agnes his widow became enamoured with Robert Duke of Normandy and attached herself in an illicit manner to him, shortly after which time his wife Sibylle died of poison."

Pope Alexander VI and his son the Duke Valentinois employed arsenic to carry out their fiendish plans, not only on their enemies, but their friends also. Thus perished by their hands the Cardinals of Capua and Modena; and Alexander himself by a cup intended for Adrian, Cardinal of Corneto, who had invited the pope to a banquet in the Vineyard of Belvedere, was destroyed instead of his host.

Lucretia Borgia, famous in romance and song for her poisoning propensities, was a daughter of Pope Alexander VI, and sister of Cesare Borgia. She married Giovanni Sforza, Lord of Pesaro, in 1493, but being a woman of haughty disposition and evil temper, their life was anything but a happy one; and after living together for four years, Alexander dissolved the marriage, and gave her to Alphonso II of Naples. Two years had barely passed before her second husband was assassinated by hired ruffians of Cesare Borgia. So Lucretia took unto herself a third husband in the person of Alphonso d'Este, a son of the Duke of Ferrara. She led a wild and unhappy life, and was accused of poisoning, and almost every form of crime, although it is stated by several modern historians that many of these charges were unfounded. Although tradition has inflicted her with a bad character, she is said to have been a liberal patroness of art and literature in her time. She died in 1523.

In 1536 the Dauphin, eldest son of Francis I, died suddenly, and suspicion attached to Sebastian Montecucculi, a Ferrarese, who held the part of cup-bearer—bribed, as was supposed by Catherine of Medicis in order to secure the crown to her husband, Henry, Duke of Orleans, who became Dauphin in consequence of his elder brother's death.

The story of the Countess of Somerset, who was tried with others for the murder of Sir Thomas Overbury in the reign of James I, forms an interesting episode in the history of romantic poisoning. Robert, Earl of Essex, son of Queen Elizabeth's favourite, and who afterwards became Commander-in-chief of the Parliamentary forces, married, at the age of fourteen, Frances Howard, a younger daughter of the Earl of Suffolk, the bride being just a year younger than her husband. The match had been arranged and brought about through the influence of relatives, who thought it expedient that the youthful bridegroom should be sent off to travel on the Continent immediately after the marriage had taken place, and he remained away for three or four years. During this period the countess, who was brought up at court, developed into a very beautiful woman, but seems to have been equally unprincipled and capricious. On the return of the earl from his travels, she shrank from all advances on his part, and showed the utmost repugnance to her husband on all occasions. Their dispositions were entirely different. He loved retirement, and wished to live a quiet country life, while she, who had been bred at court, and accustomed to adulation and intrigue, refused to leave town. The King about this time had a number of young men of distinguished appearance and good looks attached to the court, and of these, one Robert Carr, at length became an exclusive favourite. Between him and the self-willed young countess there sprang up an attachment, which, at least on her side, amounted to infatuation. Her opportunities for meeting her lover were short and rare, and in this emergency she applied to a Mrs. Turner, who introduced her to Dr. Forman, a noted astrologer and magician at that time, and he, by images made of wax, and other devices of the black art, undertook to procure the love of Carr to the lady. At the same time he was also to practise against the earl in the opposite direction. These measures, however, were too slow for the wayward countess, and having gone to the utmost lengths with her inamorata, she insisted on a divorce, and a legal marriage with him.

One of Carr's greatest friends was Sir Thomas Overbury, a young courtier and a man of honour and kindly disposition. He was much against this intimacy, and besought his friend to break it off, assuring him it would ruin his prospects and reputation if he married the lady. Carr unwisely made this known to the countess, who at once regarded Overbury as a bitter enemy, and resolved to do what she could to overthrow him. The pair plotted together with evident success, for the unfortunate Sir Thomas was shortly afterwards committed to the Tower by an arbitrary mandate of the King; next, he was not allowed to see any visitors; and, finally, his food was poisoned, and, after several unsuccessful attempts on his life, he at last died from the effects of poison. Cantharides, nitrate of silver, spiders, arsenic, and last of all, corrosive sublimate, are said to have been administered in turn to this unfortunate individual. Meanwhile, the countess obtained a divorce from her husband on the ground of impotency, and married Carr, who was soon after made Earl of Somerset by King James.

Two years elapsed before the murder of Sir Thomas Overbury was brought to light, when the inferior criminals, Mrs. Turner and the others, were convicted and executed; but the Earl of Somerset and his countess, although found guilty with their accomplices, received the royal pardon. The happiness of the earl and countess, however, was not of long duration, as it is stated they afterwards became so alienated from each other, that they resided for years under the same roof with the most careful precautions that they might not by any chance come into each other's presence. The Mrs. Turner implicated in the crime is said to have been the first to introduce into England the yellow starch that was then applied to ladies' ruffs. Her last request was, that she should be hanged in a ruff dyed with her own yellow starch, which is said to have been carried out.

According to some historians, Robert Dudley, Earl of Leicester, Prime Minister and favourite of Queen Elizabeth, was a poisoner of the most diabolical description.

His ambition to marry his royal mistress, who, shrewd woman as she was, seems to have had no insight into his unscrupulous character, was the cause of his moving every human obstacle from his path by insidious methods. The murder of his wife Amy Robsart was the first of a long series of murders, carried out, doubtless, at his instigation. He was next suspected of causing the death of Lord Sheffield, of whose lady he was an admirer. The Earl of Essex is said to have been another victim. His death is described in the language of the time as having been due to "an extreme flux caused by an Italian Receit, the maker whereof was a surgeon that then was newly come to my Lord from Italy, a cunning man and sure in operation. The inventor of this recipe was known as one Dr. Julio, who was said to be able to make a man dye in what manner of sickness you will." The death of the Earl of Essex took place when on his way home from Ireland, with the object of revenging himself on the Earl of Leicester for his domestic wrongs. The next victim is said to have been Cardinal Chatillian, who, having accused the earl of preventing the marriage of the queen to the King of France, was journeying back to Dover, when he was taken suddenly ill and died in Canterbury.

Sir Nicholas Throgmorton, a wealthy city magnate and a tool of the earl's, whom, 'tis said, he used to thwart the doings of the Lord Treasurer, Sir William Cecil, was another victim. Having heard that Sir Nicholas was revealing some of his secrets, he invited him one night to supper at his house in London, and at supper time hurriedly went to the court, to which he said he had been called suddenly by her Majesty. Sir Nicholas proceeded with the meal in his absence, and soon after was seized with a violent vomiting, from which he never recovered. According to an old chronicler, "The day before his death he declared to a dear friend, all the circumstances and cause of his complaint, which he affirmed plainly to be poison given him in a sallet at supper, inveighing most earnestly against the earl's cruelty and bloody disposition, and affirming him to be the wickedest, most perilous and perfidious man under heaven."

The chronicler continues: "And for his art of poisoning, it is such now, and reaching so far, as he holdeth all his foes in England and elsewhere, as also a good many of his friends, in fear thereof, and if it were known how many he hath despatched in that way would be marvellous to posterity.

"His body physician, one Dr. Bayly, openly proclaimed the fact that he knew of poisons which might be so tempered that they should kill the party afterwards at what time it should be appointed; which argument belike," says the writer of *Leycester's Commonwealth*, "pleased well his Lordship of Leicester. The tool who carried out the murder of the Earl of Essex is said to have been one Crompton, Yeoman of the Bottles, together with Godwick Lloyd." Leicester was suspected of being the instigator of many murders which probably he may have had nothing to do with, such was the feeling of dislike against him. Among others was Lady Lennox, who died in a mysterious manner shortly after being visited by the earl.

He is said to have kept in his employ several needy but unscrupulous physicians, ready to administer the "Italian Comfortive," as the poison was called, at his bidding. "With the Earl of Essex, one Mrs. Alice Drakott, a godly gentlewoman, is also said to have been poisoned." This lady happened to be accompanying the earl on her way towards her own house, when after partaking of the same cup she was also seized with violent pain and vomiting, which continued until she died, a day or two before the earl succumbed. "When she was dead," says the chronicler, "her body was swollen into a monstrous bigness and deformity; whereof the good earl, hearing the day following, lamented the case greatly, and said in the presence of his servants,

'Ah! poor Alice, the cup was not prepared for thee, albeit it was thy hard fortune to taste thereof.'"

_____

CHAPTER IV

THE criminal destruction of life by poison has been practised from ancient times. Very little was known of toxicology in those days, and even the symptoms often passed unrecognised or were attributed to natural causes, and the poisoners' fiendish work was frequently undiscovered and rendered easy. In the early Christian era, poisoning, indeed, became quite a profession, and convenient individuals could be hired with little difficulty to administer a deadly dose to an enemy or rival. Agrippina, in refusing to eat some apples offered to her at table by her father-in-law Tiberius, must have had suspicions of this kind. Locusta, who is said to have supplied the poison by which Agrippina got rid of Claudius, and who also prepared the dose for Britannicus, according to the order of his brother Nero, is the first professional poisoner of whom we have record.

In the year B.C. 331 an epidemic broke out in Rome which was supposed to proceed from corrupt air, but it was observed that the principal patricians only were the victims. Their deaths, however, were attributed to infection, for poisoning was then scarcely known in Rome nor was there a law for its punishment. In the general grief, a female slave presented herself to the edile curule Q. Fabius and accused more than twenty Roman ladies of poisoning: designing specially Cornelia, a lady of an illustrious family of that name, and Sergia, another patrician lady. It is recorded that as many as three hundred and sixty-six ladies were similarly accused; but Cornelia and Sergia were detected in compounding their fatal potions. "When led before the popular assembly they maintained their preparations were harmless remedies. The slave, seeing herself accused as a false witness, asked that the ladies should be required to swallow their own potions; which they did, and by so doing avoided a more shameful death."

Later, there were, doubtless, many, both men and women of the baser sort, who professed to practise alchemy, and had dealings in the black arts, who for suitable consideration would procure poison for criminal purposes. In mediæval times a law was passed in Italy rendering the apothecary, who knowingly sold poison for criminal purposes, liable to a heavy penalty, and yet secret poisoning was practised to a very large extent; and there were probably many like the poor apothecary of Mantua in *Romeo and Juliet*, who, in response to Romeo's demand for poison, replied, "My poverty and not my will consents."

From the fifteenth to the seventeenth century two great criminal schools arose in Venice and Italy.

The Venetian poisoners who first came into notoriety, flourished in the fifteenth century. At that period the mania for poisoning had risen to such a height, that the governments of the states were formally recognizing secret assassination by poison, and considering the removal of emperors, princes, and powerful nobles by this method. The notorious Council of Ten met to consider such plans, and an account and record of their proceedings still exists, giving the number of those who voted for and who voted against the proposed removal, the reasons for the assassination, and the sum to be paid for its execution. Thus these conspirators quietly arranged to take the lives of many prominent individuals; and when the deed was executed, it was registered on the margin of their official record by the significant word "Factum." On December 15, 1543, John of Raguba, a Franciscan brother, offered the Council a selection of poisons, and declared himself ready to remove any person whom they deemed objectionable out of the way. He calmly stated his terms, which for the first successful case were to be a pension of 1,500 ducats a year, to be increased on the execution of future services. The Presidents, Guolando Duoda and Pietro Guiarini, placed this matter before the Council on January 4, 1544, and on a division, it was resolved to accept this patriotic offer, and to experiment first on the Emperor Maximilian. John, who had evidently reduced poisoning to a fine art, submitted afterwards a regular graduated tariff to the Council, which ran as follows—

> For the great Sultan, 500 ducats.
> For the King of Spain, 150 ducats, including the expenses of the journey, etc.
> For the Duke of Milan, 60 ducats.
> For the Marquis of Mantua, 50 ducats.
> For the Pope, 100 ducats.

He further adds at the foot of the document, "The farther the journey, the more eminent the man, the more it is necessary to reward the toil and hardships undertaken, and the heavier must be the payment."

The school of Italian poisoners became prominent in the sixteenth and seventeenth centuries, and the magnitude of their operations during that period struck terror into the hearts of the chief nobles and rulers of that country.

The mania for secret poisoning seems to have seized on all classes from the highest to the lowest, and no one who made an enemy was safe. Porta, in his work published in 1589, gives some account of the poisons used at the time, and seems to have made a study of the subject. He describes methods for drugging wine (a favourite medium of administration) with belladonna root, and also mentions nux vomica, aconite, and hellebore, in his account of poisonous bodies. He gives the following recipe for compounding a very strong poison, which he calls "Venenum Lupinum": "Take of the powdered leaves of *Aconitum lycoctonum, Taxus baccata,* with powdered glass, caustic lime, sulphide of arsenic, and bitter almonds. Mix them with honey, and make into pills the size of a hazel nut." He also recommends a curious mixture to poison a sleeping person. It is composed of a mixture of hemlock juice, bruised stramonium, belladonna, and opium. This is to be placed in a leaden box with a perfectly fitting cover, and allowed to ferment for several days; it is then to be opened under the nose of the intended victim while asleep. So long as the individual only got the smell and did not swallow the compound, it certainly would not do him much harm.

The most notorious of the Italian poisoners was the woman Toffana or Toffania, who carried on her practices from the latter end of the seventeenth century until she was brought to justice in 1709. Toffana resided first at Palermo, but removed to Naples in 1659 during the pontificate of Alexander VII. This later Circe gained large sums of money by the sale of certain mysterious preparations she compounded, which were afterwards proved to be simply solutions of arsenious acid. These were circulated throughout Italy in small glass phials, bearing the image of a saint, and labelled various names such as "Acquetta di Napoli," or the "Manna of St. Nicholas of Bari," and "Aqua Toffana." Any one in the secret could buy the poison for its supposed use as a cosmetic, or other innocent property, and then employ it for any purpose they wished. This infamous woman carried on her nefarious trade from girlhood until she was nearly seventy years of age, without ever having fallen into the meshes of the law, and it is stated over six hundred persons were poisoned through her instrumentality. She dealt only with individuals, after due safeguards had been built up, and she changed her abode so frequently, and adopted so many disguises, that her detection was rendered very difficult. She also called in the aids of religion and superstition, and those who were uninitiated in the history of her deadly elixir, imagined it to be a certain miraculous oil which was supposed to ooze from the tomb of St. Nicholas. The Popes Pius III and Clement XIV are said to have fallen victims to its use. The composition of the Acquetta di Napoli was long a profound secret, but it is said to have been known by the Emperor Charles VI of Austria. According to a letter addressed to Hoffmann[2] by Garceli, physician to the emperor, he informed the latter that, being Governor of Naples at the time that the Acquetta was the dread of every noble family in the city, and when the subject was investigated legally he had an opportunity of examining all the documents, and that he found the poison consisted of a solution of arsenic in *Aqua cymbalariæ*. The dose was said to be from four to six drops in water, and that it was colourless, transparent and tasteless. When the manufacture and sale of the poison was at last traced to Toffana, she took refuge in a convent, from which the abbess and archbishop refused to give her up, and so continued to sell the water for twenty years longer, and evaded punishment for the time. Public indignation was roused to such a pitch, that at last the convent was broken into by a body of soldiers, who secured Toffana and handed her over to the authorities. She was tortured until she confessed in 1709, and then strangled, her body being thrown into the garden of the convent which had sheltered her.

Aqua Toffana was reputed to possess some very peculiar properties, and, among others, that of causing death at any determinate period, after months, for example, or even years of ill-health (a common supposition attributed to poisons in the Middle Ages). Its alleged effects are graphically described by Behrens as follows: "A certain indescribable change is felt in the whole body, which leads the person to complain to his physician. The physician examines and reflects, but finds no symptoms either external or internal, no vomiting, no inflammation, no fever. In short, he can only advise patience, strict regimen, and laxatives. The malady, however, creeps on, and the physician is again sent for. Still he cannot detect any symptoms of note. Meanwhile the poison takes firmer hold of the system; languor, wearisomeness, and loathing of food continue; the nobler organs gradually become torpid, and the lungs in particular at length begin to suffer. In a word, the malady from the first is incurable; the unhappy victim pines away insensibly even in the hands of the physician, and thus is he brought to a miserable end through months or years, according to his enemy's desire."

Toffana had many imitators, and some time after her death a similar scheme was attempted with a poisonous solution reputedly sold as a cosmetic, called the "Acquetta di Perugia." It is said to have been prepared by killing a hog, disjointing it, strewing the pieces with white arsenic, which was well rubbed in, and finally collecting the juice which dropped from the meat itself. This preparation was supposed to be much stronger and a more powerful poison than arsenic itself, but doubtless had the same fatal effect.

It is a curious fact that most of the notorious poisoners in mediæval times were women, and, indeed, in later years the frail sex seem to have retained a special predilection for this form of crime. In the year 1659, a secret society of women, most of whom were young wives belonging to some of the best and wealthiest families of Rome, was discovered in that city, the sole or chief object of which was to destroy the lives of the husbands of the members.

They met at regular intervals at the house of one Hieronyma Spara, a woman reputed to be a witch, who provided her fellow associates and pupils with the required poison, and planned and instructed them how to use it. Operations had been carried on for some time, when the existence of the society was discovered and, says a chronicler, "the hardened old hag passed the ordeal of the rack without confession; but another woman divulged the secrets of the sisterhood, and La Spara, together with twelve other women implicated, were hanged." Many others who were guilty in a lesser degree were publicly whipped through the streets of the city.

In the seventeenth century the mania for poisoning seems to have spread to France, and great interest was excited by the disclosures which followed the discovery of Exili's conspiracy to poison a number of persons. Madame de Montespan, one of the favourites of Louis XIV, a woman of great beauty, died very suddenly at the age of twenty-six, on June 30, 1672, and it was generally believed she had been poisoned. The rumour seems to have been set on foot by one of her husband's old servants, who professed to know the individual who had administered the fatal dose. "This man," said he, "who was not rich, withdrew immediately afterwards into Normandy, where he bought an estate, on which he lived with grandeur a long time; the poison was powder of diamonds, mixed, instead of sugar, with strawberries."

Voltaire, who believed the whole story to be a myth, states: "The court and city believed the princess had been poisoned with a glass of water of succory, after which she felt terrible pains, and soon after was seized with the agonies of death; but the natural malignity of mankind, and a fondness for extraordinary incidents, were the only inducements to this general persuasion. The glass of water could not be poisoned, since Madame de la Fayette and another person drunk what remained without receiving the least injury from it. The princess had been a long time ill of an abscess, which had formed itself in the liver." For some time the young Chevalier De Lorraine, the favourite of the Duke of Orleans, rested under suspicion, it being openly stated that the motive was to revenge the banishment and imprisonment which his misbehaviour to the princess a short time before had drawn upon him. Public opinion was strengthened in the belief that the princess had met her death through poison, by the fact that just at this time the mania for secret poisoning seemed to spread over France. About this date a German apothecary and alchemist, named Glaser, settled in Paris, together with two Italians, one of whom was called Exili. Their professed object was a research to discover the Philosopher's Stone. Having lost the little they possessed in a very short time in the pursuit of this chimera, they commenced the secret sale of poisons. Through the confessional their nefarious trade became known to the Grand Penitentiary of Paris. This dignitary gave information to the Government, and the two suspected Italians were promptly sent to the Bastille, where one of them died; but Exili, while still in prison, managed to carry on his business, and found ready purchasers for his secrets, and the number of deaths attributed to poison increased to such an extent, that a special court for the investigation of poisoning cases, called "La Chambre Ardente," was formed. A few years later the whole of France was aroused by the confession of the Marquise de Brinvilliers of having poisoned her father, two brothers, and a sister. Her husband, the Marquis de Brinvilliers, invited a friend, one Captain St. Croix, who was an officer in his regiment, to lodge in his house. The too agreeable person of the lady of the house speedily charmed the visitor, and to her credit she endeavoured to inspire her husband with a fear of the consequences; but he obstinately persisted in keeping his young friend in the house with his wife, who was both young and handsome, with the result they soon conceived a passion for each other. The father of the marquise, one Lieutenant Daubrai was greatly incensed on hearing of his daughter's indiscretions, and obtaining a *lettre de cachet* had the captain sent to the Bastille. Here St. Croix was placed in the same cell as Exili, and the latter soon instructed him how he might easily revenge himself. The marquise, who found means of visiting her lover, was informed how to obtain the poison, and at once commenced operations on those members of her family who were most incensed against her, with the result, that first her father, then her brothers and sister fell victims to her revenge. Suspicion resting on her, she fled into Belgium, and was arrested at Liège. A full confession of her crimes, written by her own hand, was found upon her.

She was eventually beheaded, and burnt near Notre Dame in July, 1676. St. Croix is said to have accidentally succumbed to the effects of poisonous fumes in his own laboratory. The authorities on examining his effects, as he left no family, came across a small box to which a paper was attached, which contained a request that after his death "it might be delivered to the Marquise de Brinvilliers, who resides in Rue Neuve St. Paul." This paper was signed and dated by St. Croix on May 25, 1672. On the box being opened, it was found to contain a large collection of various poisons, including corrosive sublimate, antimony, and opium. When the marquise heard of the death of her lover, she at once made every effort to obtain the box by bribing the officers of justice, but failed. La Chaussée, the servant of St. Croix, laid claim to the property, but was arrested as an accomplice and imprisoned. On confessing many serious crimes he was broken alive on the wheel in 1673. Evidence was brought to prove at the trial of De Brinvilliers, that both she and St. Croix were secretly combined with other persons accused of similar crimes. Some distinguished people were implicated, including Pennautier, the receiver- general of the clergy, who was afterwards accused of practising her secrets.

One crime seemed to bring another to light, and two persons, named La Voisin and La Vigoreux, a priest named Le Sage, and several others, were next haled before the tribunal, and charged with trading with the secrets of Exili and inciting people with weak minds to the crime of poisoning. It was alleged that through their instrumentality a large number of married women had hastened the decease of their husbands.

The Chambre Ardente, or Burning Court, as it was commonly called, was established at the Arsenal, near the Bastille, and was rarely idle. Persons of the highest rank were cited to appear before it; among others, two nieces of Cardinal Mazarin, the Duchess of Bouillon, and the Countess de Soissons, mother of Prince Eugène. The Countess de Soissons had to retire to Brussels.

The Marshal de Luxemburg was the next sensational arrest. He was carried to the Bastille and submitted to a long examination, after which he was allowed to remain fourteen months in prison. La Voisin and his accomplices were eventually condemned and burnt at the stake, which seemed to put a check on this series of abominable crimes which spread throughout France from 1670 to 1680.

Maria Louisa, daughter of Louis XIV, who married Charles II, King of Spain, is said to have died from the effects of poison in 1689. Voltaire states: "It was undoubtedly believed that the Austrian Ministers of Charles II would get rid of her, because she loved her country and might prevent the king, her husband, from declaring for the allies against France; they even sent her from Versailles what they believed to be a counter-poison." This did not arrive until after her death. In the memoirs of the Marquis de Dangeau, he says: "The king announced the death of his daughter at supper in these words—'The Queen of Spain is dead, poisoned by eating of an eel pye; and the Countess de Pernits and the Cameras, Zapeita, and Nina, who eat of it after her, are also dead of the same poison.'" It is more than probable the unfortunate queen and her ladies succumbed to some putrefactive poison in the fish itself, and were not killed by intent. Nothing was known of animal poisons in those days, and such was the state of the public mind that nearly every sudden death was at once attributed to poison.

The close of the reign of Louis XIV was marked by the sudden deaths of no less than six members of the royal family in close succession. The public sorrow and excitement were great, and rumours and suspicions of poisoning were revived with fury unexampled. The prince had a laboratory, and among other arts studied chemistry. This was considered by the ignorant to be sufficient proof, and the public outcry became terrible. On a visit of the Marquis de Canellae, the prince was found extended on the floor shedding tears, and distracted with despair. His chemist and fellow worker, Homberg, ran to surrender himself at the Bastille, but they refused to receive him without orders. The prince was so beside himself on hearing the public outcry and suspicions that he demanded to be put in prison so that his innocence might be cleared by judicial forms. The *lettre de cachet* was actually made out, but not signed. The marquis alone kept his head, and prevailed upon the prince's mother to oppose the *lettre de cachet*. "The monarch who granted it, and his nephew who demanded it, were both equally wretched," says the historian.

The "poudre de succession," famous in Paris as a secret poison, was at one time supposed to consist of diamond dust, but, according to Haller, was really composed of sugar of lead. This was used by several notorious criminals during the seventeenth century.

[2] Hoffmann, *Medecina Rationalis Systematica*, i. 198.

CHAPTER V

THE use of poison as an instrument for political purposes during the Middle Ages soon spread over Europe, and the dread of wholesale poisoning caused numerous panics. Some of these alarms may probably have been circulated by unscrupulous traders who had articles to sell, or some business interest to forward, but of others authentic records exist.

June 6 is still kept as a public holiday in Malta. Upon that day, a century and a half ago, while the island was still possessed by the Knights of St. John, a Jew waited on the Grand Master, and revealed to him a plot that had been planned for exterminating the whole population at a stroke. This man kept a coffee house frequented by the Turkish slaves, and understanding their language, he had overheard suspicious remarks among his customers. The Grand Master, believing the truth of the man's statement, took immediate action. The slaves indicated were at once seized and put to torture, and they confessed a design of poisoning all the wells and fountains on the island, and to make the result surer, each of the conspirators was to assassinate a Christian. One hundred and twenty-five were found guilty. Some were burnt, some broken on the wheel, while others were ordered to have their arms and legs attached to two galleys which, on being rowed apart, would thus dismember them. Whether these frightful punishments were carried out it is impossible to say, but the fact remains that the people of Malta still commemorate their escape from poisoning to the present time.

Wholesale poisoning appears to have been a common practice in Eastern countries, especially in India and Persia. The wells or other water sources were usually chosen as the medium for disseminating the poison, and in this way whole villages have often been destroyed by some miscreant. Another extraordinary poisoning plot was discovered in Lima towards the close of the eighteenth century. During the insurrection of 1781, a rich Cacique, who professed loyalty, went to a chemist's shop and asked for 200 lb. of corrosive sublimate. He was willing to pay any price. The chemist had not anything like that amount in stock, and not wishing to send such a good customer away, substituted 200 lb. of alum. On the following day all the water in the town was found to be impregnated with alum. An examination being made of the reservoir, it was found that the fence round it had been broken down and the banks strewn with alum, and the water rendered undrinkable.

England has remained practically free from crimes of this kind. In 1530, a case occurred which caused great public indignation. Fisher, Bishop of

Rochester, was accustomed to entertain a number of poor people daily. One afternoon a large number of his humble guests, together with some of the officers of the household, were taken ill. Two died, and after an examination of the food had been made, it was declared the yeast had been poisoned. Parliament took up the investigation, and the bishop's cook, one Richard Rowe, was found guilty. He was tried, and sentenced to be boiled alive as a terrible example to others. Boiling seems to have been a favourite punishment for poisoners during the Middle Ages, a fact which, doubtless, shows the abhorrence in which crimes of this kind were held.

It is further recorded that "On March 17th, 1524, Margaret Davy, maid, was boiled in Smithfield for poisoning three households she had dwelled in."

Among Queen Elizabeth's statesmen, poison would appear to have been regarded as almost a legitimate weapon of defence. Her favourite Leicester, to whom we have already alluded, was often called "The Poisoner." This propensity was probably largely due to the fact that most young Englishmen of rank were sent to Italy to finish their education, and there were introduced to the Italian methods of poisoning so much in vogue.

The Duc de Guise, in his memoirs, relates in a most matter-of-fact way, how he requested the captain of his guard to poniard a troublesome demagogue at Naples. The captain was shocked. He would poison any one at his Grace's command with pleasure, but the dagger was a vulgar instrument. So the duke bought some strong poison, the composition of which he describes at length, and it was duly administered. But Gennaro, the intended victim, had just eaten cabbage dressed in oil, which is said to have acted as an antidote, and so he lived after all.

CHAPTER VI

CONCERNING ARSENIC

ARSENIC has, perhaps, been more frequently used than any other poison for criminal purposes. It was known to the ancient Greeks in the form of the yellow sulphide, commonly called orpiment. It is found in Greece and Hungary. Its bright yellow colour caused many of the early alchemists to consider it the key to the Philosopher's Stone, and this is said to be grounded on some enigmatical verse in the Sibylline oracles. The Emperor Caligula, according to Pliny, ordered a great quantity of orpiment to be melted and manipulated, so that the gold it was supposed to contain might be extracted from it.

Arsenic is the agent most commonly employed for criminal purposes in India, doubtless because it can be both easily and cheaply obtained. The reports of the analyst to the Bombay Government threw considerable light on the methods pursued by Indian poisoners. The poison is usually given in sweetmeats, and generally by a "strange woman," who has been met in the street and who mysteriously disappears. This "strange woman" is found in every analyst's report for the past twenty years, and under much the same circumstances. Most of the cases are typical of the people among whom they occur, as, for instance, the following:

"In a Scinde district a man went into a shop one day and entered into friendly conversation with a stranger he met there. On parting, by way of thanking him, the stranger presented him with some sweets for distribution among his friends. The result was that five men and a boy were poisoned, and the obliging stranger has never been heard of since."

The professional poisoner in India—for there are many such—is rarely caught or even suspected. In a large number of cases, crimes of this kind are taken little notice of by the community; and sometimes the poisoner apparently thinks nothing of poisoning a whole family in order to make sure of his victim. The utter absence of motive in the majority of cases would point to the conclusion that they were largely the result of homicidal mania.

For more than a century after the properties of arsenic were well known, there was no certain method known for its detection, and very little advance was made until the early part of last century, when Marsh discovered his test in 1836, by means of which the minutest quantities of the poison may be detected.

It is characteristic of both arsenic and mercury, that their presence may be proved and demonstrated, even in the bones, years after they have been taken. In proof of this, the following remarkable case is given. A wealthy farmer died, and was buried in the tomb where his father had been interred thirty-five years before. An examination of certain of the bones of the father revealed particles of a metallic-looking substance, which was collected and tested, and proved to be mercury. It had thus been preserved in his body for more than the third of a century, the probability being, that he had been in the habit of taking it medicinally during the latter part of his life. Another strange case came under the notice of a Bristol chemist, in which he found abundant traces of arsenic in the bodies of several young children after they had been buried eight years.

A curious story is related by the late Sir Richard Quain that came under his experience, and one which would have proved a profound mystery to this day but for his practical knowledge and acumen. He was asked to make a post-mortem examination on the body of a man who was by trade a stone-mason. To continue the story in his own words, "One day, on coming in to his dinner, he went into the scullery, washed his hands, and, going into the kitchen, he said to his wife, 'It is all over; I have taken poison.' 'What have you taken?' 'Arsenic,' he replied, and she at once took him off to the Western General Dispensary. The senior surgeon was out when they got there, but two young pupils of his happened to be in, who thought it was a very important case, and they would treat it pretty actively. So they gave him tartar emetic, pumped out the stomach, and pumped oxide of iron into it, and a good many other operations they performed. The poor man was extremely ill, and died in twenty-four hours. The coroner's beadle went to the chemist and said: 'How did you come to sell this man poison?' He replied, 'I sold him no poison; I thought he was off his head when he came.' 'What did you give him?' 'Oh, I gave him some alum and cream of tartar and labelled it poison.' He swallowed this, in the belief it was arsenic," says Sir Richard. "When I made the post-mortem examination, to my amazement I found a great deal of *arsenic* in the stomach. This was rather puzzling. I said, if it is in the stomach it ought to go farther down. So I searched the intestines, but there was no trace of arsenic anywhere. The simple explanation of it was this, these two young fellows, horrified to find the man had died without taking arsenic after all, pumped some into the stomach."

Another instance that terminated in a less tragic manner, in which a would-be suicide was frustrated by a watchful chemist, happened some years ago.

One morning a tall, decently dressed man, of seafaring aspect, entered a chemist's shop in the neighbourhood of the docks of a northern seaport, and in a solemn and confidential manner asked for a shilling's worth of *strong* laudanum.

"For what purpose do you require it?" asked the chemist.

"Well, you see, sir," the man explained, "I've just come off a voyage from 'Frisco, and I find my sweetheart has gone off with Jim, you see, sir, and now it's all up with me. Give me a strong dose, please, and if you don't think a shilling's worth will be enough——"

"But, my good man——" interrupted the chemist.

"I'll shoot myself if not, sir, I will."

"All right, then," said the chemist; and, seeing argument was useless, he proceeded to mix an innocent but nauseous draught of aloes.

"Now put in a shilling's worth of arsenic."

"Very well," replied the chemist, adding some harmless magnesia.

"And you might as well throw in a shilling's worth of prussic acid," said the broken-hearted lover.

The chemist carefully measured a little essence of almonds into the glass, and handed it to the would-be suicide. He paid, swallowed it at one draught, and solemnly walked out of the shop.

Crossing the street, which was quiet at the time, he deliberately laid himself flat on his back on the footpath, and closed his eyes.

A group of children gathered round, and stood gazing with their eyes and mouths open in wonderment, and an occasional passer-by stopped a moment, cast a glance at the unwonted sight, and then passed on.

After lying thus quite motionless for about five minutes, he suddenly raised his head, took a look round, then with one bound jumped to his feet and made off as hard as he could run.

It is a curious fact that arsenic has been the favourite medium of female poisoners from very early times; and in two celebrated poisoning cases of later years, in both of which women were accused of murder by the administration of arsenic, the plea that the poison had been used by them for cosmetic purposes has been put forward to account for having it in their possession. The effect of arsenic on the skin is well known, and that it is frequently used, both internally and externally, to improve the skin, by women, is an undoubted fact.[3] That such a practice may lead to the taking of arsenic as a confirmed habit there is also evidence to prove, and the writer has met with more than one instance, in which the habit of taking solution of arsenic in large quantities has been contracted by women.

[3] The recent rage for the so-called arsenical soaps, which are supposed to improve the complexion and are being extensively used by women, goes to corroborate this statement.

CHAPTER VII

THE STRANGE CASE OF MADAME LAFARGE

THE story of Madame Lafarge, who was tried in France for the murder of her husband in 1840, is a strangely romantic one.

Marie Fortunée Cappelle was the daughter of a captain in the Imperial Artillery. Her parents died in her childhood, and she was placed in the care of an aunt, who, at the earliest opportunity, determined to relieve herself of the burden of her support by negotiating a marriage for her. While still a girl, through the instrumentality of a matrimonial agent in Paris, an alliance was arranged between Marie Cappelle and one Monsieur Charles Lafarge, who was a widower and an ironmaster of Glandier.

The marriage, which was purely a commercial transaction, took place in Paris on August 15, 1839, after which, Lafarge and his young wife set out for his old and gloomy seigneurial mansion in Glandier.

From statements made afterwards, Madame Lafarge became disgusted with her husband's brutality before the honeymoon was over. After they reached their own house, however, they were reconciled, and there seemed to be every possibility of their spending a happy wedded life together.

Besides the newly married pair, there lived in the family mansion the mother and sister of Lafarge, and his chief clerk, one Denis Barbier, was a frequent visitor at the house, and had liberty to walk through the place without restriction.

In a very short time Madame Lafarge discovered that both she and her relatives had been deceived as to the position of her husband, and that instead of being a man of considerable fortune, he was straitened for means. On his representations she bestowed upon him all her fortune, and even wrote letters at his dictation to some of her wealthy friends, asking them to aid him to find money to develop a new method he claimed to have discovered for smelting iron. With these letters of introduction, Lafarge set out for Paris in December, 1839, to raise money to start his new project.

While he was thus away, his wife had her portrait drawn by an artist in Glandier, and determined to send it to her absent husband. She therefore packed it in a box, with some cakes made by his mother, together with an affectionate letter, and despatched them to Paris. This box, which contained nothing but the five small cakes, the portrait, and the letter, was packed and sealed by Madame Lafarge in the presence of several witnesses.

When it reached Paris and was opened by Lafarge, it contained only *one large cake*, after partaking of which he was suddenly taken ill, and was eventually compelled to return home, where he arrived on January 5, 1840. His sickness continued and increased in severity, and nine days afterwards he died.

Shortly after his death his mother and friends, who were well aware how the widow disliked them and her husband also, whc had made her life so unhappy, at once imputed the cause of death to poison administered by his wife in the cake she had sent to Paris, and Marie Cappelle Lafarge was arrested on suspicion.

When the house of the deceased man was searched, certain diamonds were found, which were supposed to have been stolen from the Vicomtesse de Léotaud by Madame Lafarge before her marriage.

The unfortunate woman was therefore charged with the double crime of theft and murder.

Though arrested in January, 1840, the trial of Madame Lafarge did not commence till July 9 of the same year, and the charge of theft was first proceeded with in her absence, and she was found guilty.

While this judgment was still under appeal, she was brought to trial on the graver charge.

The evidence for the prosecution went to prove that the illness of Lafarge commenced with the eating of the cake received from his home. As already stated, when the box arrived in Paris the seals had been broken, the five cakes had disappeared, and *a single cake "as large as a plate"* had been substituted for them. It was alleged by the prosecution that this single cake had been prepared by Madame Lafarge, and secretly placed in the box; but no evidence could be brought to prove that she ever tampered with the box after it had been sealed. Lafarge's clerk, Denis Barbier, made a clandestine visit to Paris after the box had been despatched, and he was with Lafarge when it arrived in Paris, yet no notice seems to have been taken of this suspicious fact. It transpired, it was he who also first threw out hints on his master's return that he was being poisoned by arsenic, and told a brother employé that his master would be dead within ten days. There was ample proof, however, that there was a considerable quantity of arsenic in the house at Glandier. It was found that Madame Lafarge had purchased some in December, stating she required it for destroying rats; Denis also stated in evidence, that Madame had requested him to procure her some arsenic. He bought some, but did not give it to her. It was further stated that Madame Lafarge was seen to stir a white powder into some chicken broth which had been prepared for her husband, the remains of which, found in a bowl, were said by the analyst to contain arsenic.

The medical men who conducted the post-mortem examination gave it as their deliberate opinion that the deceased man had been poisoned by arsenic, of which metal they professed to have found considerable quantities. The friends of the accused then submitted the matter to Orfila, the famous toxicologist, who, on giving his opinion of the methods and manner in which the analysis had been carried out, said that owing to the antiquated and doubtful methods of detection employed by the medical men, it was probable they fancied they had found arsenic where there was none. Thereupon the prosecution asked Orfila to undertake a fresh analysis himself, which he consented to do, and, on making a careful examination of the remains, stated he discovered just a minute trace of arsenic.

This apparently sealed the doom of the accused woman, and served to strengthen the bias of the jury. But now another actor appeared in the drama in the person of Raspail, another famous French chemist, who had watched the case from the beginning with interest. On hearing the result of Orfila's examination, he had taken the trouble to trace the zinc wire with which Orfila had experimented, to the shop where the great toxicologist had procured the article, and he found on analysis that the *zinc itself* contained more arsenic than Orfila had detected by his examination. Orfila had used Marsh's test, which is infallible so long as the reagents used are free from arsenic themselves.

Raspail, having placed the result of his discovery of arsenic in Orfila's reagent, at the service of the defence, was on his way to Tulle, where the Assizes were being held, when an unfortunate accident delayed his progress, and the unhappy Marie Cappelle Lafarge, after a trial which lasted sixteen days, was found guilty meanwhile, and condemned to imprisonment for life with hard labour, and exposure in the pillory. Raspail, however, would not let the matter rest, and at once set to work to save the condemned woman. He at length got Orfila to fairly admit his error and join him in a professional report to the authorities to that effect.

After being imprisoned for twelve years, in the end the sentence on this unhappy woman was reduced to five years in the Montpellier house of detention, after which the Government sent her to the Convent of St. Rémy, from whence she was liberated in 1852, but only to end her wretched life a few months afterwards.

There appeared in the *Edinburgh Review* for 1842 a careful examination of this interesting case from a legal point of view, in which the writer states the strongest evidence indicated Denis and not Madame Lafarge as the perpetrator of the crime. It was proved this man lived by forgery, and assisted

Lafarge in some very shady transactions to cover the latter's insolvency. He was further known to harbour a deadly hatred for Madame Lafarge. He was with his master in Paris when he was seized with the sudden illness, and it transpired that out of the 25,000 francs the ironmaster had succeeded in borrowing from his wife's relatives, only 3,900 could be found when he returned to Glandier. On his own statement he was in the possession of a quantity of arsenic, and he was the first to direct suspicion against his master's wife. Yet all these facts appear to have been overlooked in the efforts of the prosecution to fasten the guilt on the unfortunate woman. That Lafarge died from the effects of arsenical poisoning there seems little doubt, but by whom it was administered has never been conclusively proved, and the tragedy still remains among the unsolved poisoning mysteries.

CHAPTER VIII

T$_{HE}$ case of Madeline Smith, who was charged with causing the death of L'Angelier by the administration of arsenic at Glasgow, in 1857, excited universal interest. Owing to the social position of the lady, the trial was a *cause célèbre* of the time, and the circumstances of the case were of an extraordinary character. Miss Smith, who was a young and accomplished woman at that time, and who resided in a fashionable quarter of Glasgow, got entangled with a French clerk named Pierre Emile L'Angelier. L'Angelier died very suddenly in an unaccountable manner, and suspicion falling on Madeline Smith, who was frequently in his company, she was arrested and charged with the crime. The Crown case was, that she poisoned her lover that she might be betrothed to a personage of high social standing. That L'Angelier died on March 23 from the effects of arsenic was amply proved, but while suspicious acts were alleged against the accused woman, no direct evidence was adduced to show that she administered the drug. The worst point against her was the fact of her having possession of the poison; and, irrespective of two previous purchases of coloured arsenic for which she had given false reasons, it was proved that the accused had purchased one ounce, as she said, "to kill rats," on March 18, only five days before the death of L'Angelier. The arsenic sold was coloured with indigo, according to the Act of Parliament. When charged with the crime, and required to account for the poison, she replied she had used the whole of it to apply to her face, arms, and neck, diluted with water, and that a school companion had told her that arsenic was good for the complexion. From the post-mortem examination and subsequent analysis *eighty-eight* grains of arsenic were found in the stomach and its contents. Dr. Christison, the greatest toxicological expert of the time, was called, and stated he knew of no case in which so much as eighty-eight grains of arsenic had been found in the stomach after death.

This was made a turning-point of the defence, and it was contended that so large a dose of arsenic could not have been swallowed unknowingly, and, therefore, suicide was indicated. The jury accepting this view of the case, returned a verdict of "not proven," and Madeline Smith was liberated, the trial having lasted ten days.

Some interesting particulars concerning the subsequent life of this lady were published some time ago. After the trial she decided to go abroad; but before starting she is said to have married a certain mysterious individual named Dr. Tudor Hora. With him she lived for many years in Perth, but few people ever saw her, and the doctor always declined to divulge his wife's maiden name. He kept a small surgery, and is said to have been in receipt of about £400 a year from an unnamed source. Some years after, believing that his wife had been recognized, he bought a practice at Hotham, near Melbourne, and they sailed for Australia. Shortly after their arrival, Mrs. Hora left her husband, and remained absent from Melbourne until his death. Soon afterwards she married again, but it is said her second union was not by any means a happy one. She remained unknown, and sought no society. She was an excellent musician, and spent most of her time in reading and playing. She had no children, and died at the age of fifty-five.

Six years after the trial of Madeline Smith a case was tried at the Chester Assizes, in which a woman named Hewitt or Holt was charged with poisoning her mother. Although the symptoms of irritant poisoning were very clearly marked, the country practitioner, who attended the woman at the time, certified that the cause of her death was gastro-enteritis. Eleven weeks after she had been buried, the body was exhumed and examined. An analysis revealed the presence of one hundred and fifty-four grains of arsenic in the stomach alone. The possession of a considerable quantity of arsenic was brought home to the accused, and also direct evidence of its administration, and she was found guilty. This case is interesting from the fact of proof being obtained of the administration of so large a quantity of arsenic, and if it had occurred before the trial of Madeline Smith it might have demolished her counsel's main line of defence.

CHAPTER IX

O_N July 31, 1889, one of the most remarkable poisoning cases of modern times was brought before Mr. Justice Stephen, at the Liverpool Assizes. The trial, which lasted eight days, excited the keenest interest throughout the country, especially as the principal actors in the tragedy were people of good social position. The accused, Florence Maybrick, wife of a Liverpool merchant, was charged with causing the death of her husband by administering arsenic to him.

About the end of April, 1889, Mr. James Maybrick was seized with a peculiar illness, of which the main symptoms consisted of a rigidity of the limbs and a general feeling of sickness, which quite prostrated him, and eventually confined him to bed. The medical man who was called in to attend him, attributed the cause to extreme irritability of the stomach and treated him accordingly; but, becoming puzzled by the persistent sickness and the rapidly increasing weakness of his patent, a second practitioner was called in consultation. From this time he grew considerably worse, severer symptoms and diarrhœa set in, which caused the doctors to suspect the cause was due to some irritant poison. This was confirmed by the discovery that arsenic had been placed in a bottle of meat juice that was being administered to the sick man. Trained nurses were placed in charge, and a close watch kept on the patient, but without avail, and he died on May 11.

Suspicions having been aroused, and from statements made to the police, Mrs. Maybrick was arrested, and eventually charged with the wilful murder of her husband. From evidence given at the trial, it transpired that the relations between husband and wife had not been of the most cordial character for some time. There were frequent disagreements, and just before Mr. Maybrick was taken ill there had been a serious quarrel, resulting from his wife's relations with another man. The lady resented the accusation, and a separation was talked of. The fatal illness then intervened, during the first portion of which Mrs. Maybrick nursed her husband; but through a letter addressed to her lover, which she had given to her nursemaid to post, having been opened by the latter and handed to Mr. Maybrick's brother, trained nurses were called in, and the sick man was placed in their charge entirely. This letter, which formed one of the strongest pieces of evidence against the accused, revealed the connection between Mrs. Maybrick and her lover, and contained the intelligence to him that her husband was "sick unto death." Evidence was also given by the servants, of flypapers having been seen in process of maceration in water in Mrs. Maybrick's bedroom. The trained nurses also gave evidence concerning the suspicious conduct of Mrs. Maybrick, with reference to tampering with the medicines and meat juice which were to be administered to the patient. These suspicions culminated in the discovery of arsenic in a bottle of the meat juice by one of the medical attendants. Considerable quantities of arsenic were found by the police in the house, including a packet containing seventy-one grains, mixed with charcoal, and labelled "Poison for cats."

The analytical examination was made by Dr. Stevenson and a local analytical chemist, who discovered traces of arsenic in the intestines, and .049 of a grain of arsenic in the liver, traces of the poison being also found in the spleen. Arsenic was also found in various medicine bottles, handkerchiefs, bottles of glycerine, and in the pocket of a dressing-gown belonging to the accused. Dr. Stevenson further stated, he believed the body of the deceased at the time of death probably contained a fatal dose of arsenic. The scientific evidence adduced was of a very conflicting character. On one hand, the medical men who attended the deceased, and the Government analyst, swore they believed that death was caused from the effects of arsenic; while on the other, Dr. Tidy, who was called for the defence, as an expert stated that the quantity of arsenic discovered in the body did not point to the fact that an overdose had been administered. He believed that death had been due to gastro-enteritis of some kind or other, but that the symptoms and post-mortem appearances distinctly pointed away from arsenic as the cause of death. Dr. MacNamara, ex-president of the Royal College of Surgeons, Ireland, also stated, that in his opinion Mr. Maybrick's death had not been caused by arsenical poisoning and that he agreed with Dr. Tidy that the cause was gastro-enteritis, unconnected with arsenical poisoning. For the defence it was also urged that the deceased man had been in the habit of taking arsenic in considerable quantities for some years. In support of this, witnesses were called to prove that he had been in the habit of taking a mysterious white powder, and that while living in America, he frequently purchased arsenic from chemists who knew he was in the habit of taking it. A black man, who had been in the service of deceased in America, also deposed to seeing him take this white powder in beef tea.

At the close of the evidence for the defence the accused woman by permission of the judge made the following statement amid the breathless silence of those in the court:—

"My Lord, I wish to make a statement, as well as I can, about a few facts in connection with the dreadful and crushing charge that has been made against me—the charge of poisoning my husband and father of my dear children. I wish principally to refer to the flypaper solution. The flypapers I bought with the intention of using the solution as a cosmetic. Before my marriage, and since for many years, I have been in the habit of using this wash for the face prescribed for me by Dr. Graves, of Brooklyn. It consisted, I believe, principally of arsenic, of tincture of benzoin, and elder-flower water, and some other ingredients. This prescription I lost or mislaid last April, and as at the time I was suffering from an eruption on the face I thought I should like to try and make a substitute myself. I was anxious to get rid of this eruption before I went to a ball on the 30th of that month. When I had been in Germany, among my young friends there, I had seen used a solution derived from flypapers soaked in elder-flower water, and then applied to the face with a handkerchief well soaked in the solution. I procured the flypapers and used them in the same manner, and to avoid evaporation I put the solution into a bottle so as to avoid as much as possible the admission of the air. For this purpose I put a plate over the flypapers, then a folded towel over that, and then another towel over that. My mother has been aware for a great many years that I have used arsenic in solution. I now wish to speak of his illness. On Thursday night, May 9, after the nurse had given my husband medicine, I went and sat on the bed beside him. He complained to me of feeling very sick, very weak, and very restless. He implored me then again to give him the powder which he had referred to earlier in the evening, and which I declined to give him. I was over-wrought, terribly anxious, miserably unhappy, and his evident distress utterly unnerved me. As he told me the powder would not harm him, and that I could put it in his food, I then consented. My Lord, I had not one true or honest friend in the house. I had no one to consult, no one to advise me. I was deposed from my own position as mistress of my own house, and from the position of attending on my husband, and notwithstanding that he was so ill, and notwithstanding the evidence of the nurses and the servants, I may say that he missed me whenever I was not with him; whenever I was out of the room he asked for me, and four days before he died I was not allowed to give him a piece of ice without its being taken out of my hand. I took the meat juice into the inner room. On going through the door I spilled some of the liquid from the bottle, and in order to make up the quantity spilled I put in a considerable quantity of water. On returning into the room I found my husband asleep. I placed the bottle on the table near the window. As he did not ask for anything then, and as I was not anxious to give him anything, I removed it from the small table where it attracted his attention and put it on the washstand where he could not see it. There I left it. Until Tuesday, May 14, the Tuesday after my husband's death, till a few moments before the terrible charge was made against me, no one in that house had informed me of the fact that a death certificate had been refused—but of course the post-mortem examination had taken place—or that there was any reason to suppose that my husband had died from other than natural causes. It was only when a witness alluded to the presence of arsenic in the meat juice that I was made aware of the nature of the powder my husband had been taking. In conclusion, I only wish to say that for the love of our children, and for the sake of their future, a perfect reconciliation had taken place between us, and on the day before his death I made a full and free confession to him."

Mrs. Maybrick's counsel, Sir Charles Russell, made a most brilliant and eloquent appeal in her defence. He pointed out that at the time the black shadow which could never be dispelled passed over the life of the accused woman, her husband was in the habit of drugging himself. She was deposed from her position as mistress of her own home, and pointed out as an object of suspicion.

If it had not been for the act of infidelity on her part, there would be no motive assigned in the case, and surely there was a wide chasm between the grave moral guilt of unfaithfulness and the criminal guilt involved in the deliberate plotting by such wicked means of the felonious death of her husband. There were two questions to be answered: Was there clear, safe, and satisfactory equivocal proof, either that death was in fact caused by arsenical poisoning, or that the accused woman administered that poison if to the poison the death of her husband was due? The jury, however, returned a verdict of "Guilty," and Florence Maybrick was sentenced to death. The agitation and excitement throughout the country which followed, ending in a respite being granted and the sentence being commuted to one of penal servitude for life, will be well remembered.

Whether Florence Maybrick did actually administer arsenic to her husband *with intent to kill him*, she alone can tell. On her own confession she admitted having given him a certain *white powder* for which he craved, of the nature of which she said she was ignorant. There can be no doubt *this powder was arsenic*. If she did not know the powder was arsenic, and did not give it with intent to take his life, which many still believe, then surely such a web of circumstantial evidence has never before been woven round one accused of having committed a terrible crime.

CHAPTER X

ACONITE, or monk's-hood, whose purple flower, shaped like a helmet or monk's hood, is a familiar feature in our country gardens, ranks as one of the most ancient of vegetable poisons. The name aconite was derived from Akon, a city of Heraclea, and the plant, owing to its deadly nature, was supposed by the early Greeks to have originated from the foam of the dog Cerberus. Aconite was largely used as an arrow poison by the ancients, and also employed for that purpose by the Chinese and the wild hill tribes of India. It was used by the ancient Greeks and Romans to destroy life, and they believed they could cause death to take place at a certain time by regulating the dose of poison. Thus Theophrastus writes: "The ordering of this poison was different according as it was designed to kill in two or three months, or a year." The poison cup of the ancients was probably a compound, of which hemlock and aconite were the chief ingredients. This was used for carrying out the criminal death penalty, and also for purposes of suicide when so desired. A curious relic of this ancient custom was practised at Marseilles, where a poison was kept by the public authorities of which hemlock was an ingredient. A dose of this was allowed by the magistrates "to any one who could show a sufficient reason why he should deserve death." Valerius Maximus observes, "This custom came from Greece, particularly from the Island of Ceos, where I saw an example of it in a woman of great quality who, having lived very happy ninety years, obtained leave to die this way, lest, by living longer, she should happen to see a change of her good fortune."

Theophrastus states, "Thrasyas, a great physician, invented a composition which would cause death without any pain, and it was prepared with the juice of hemlock and poppy together, and did the business in a small dose."

When vice and dissipation were at their height in Rome, suicide was most common, and it was often met with among the Greeks, after they had been contaminated by Roman manners and customs. When the Greeks and Romans recognised the impossibility of suppressing suicide, they decided to establish tribunals, whose duty it should be to hear the applications of those persons who wished to die. If the applicant succeeded in showing what the tribunal considered good cause for quitting life his prayer was granted, and he destroyed himself under the authority of the court. In some instances the court not only sanctioned the suicide, but supplied the means of self-destruction in the shape of a decoction of aconite and hemlock. If any one applied for permission to end his life and was refused, and in defiance of the decision committed suicide, his act was illegal. The Romans in such cases confiscated the property of the deceased; the Greeks held his memory as dishonoured, and treated his body with indignity.

The aconite now used in medicine is derived from the *Aconitum napellus*, chiefly grown in Britain; it is also found in the mountainous districts of the temperate parts of the northern hemisphere. It grows on the Alps, the Pyrenees, the mountains of Germany and Austria, and also in Denmark and Sweden. On the Himalayas it is found at 10,000 to 16,000 feet above the sea level. Both the root and the leaves are used medicinally. The tap root of the aconite has been frequently eaten in mistake for horse-radish with fatal results. Aconite contains several active principles, all of which are powerful poisons. The chief of these is aconitine—probably the most deadly poison known—the fiftieth part of a grain of which has nearly caused death. Indian aconite, known as *Bish*, is chiefly derived from *Aconitum ferox*—a native of high altitude in the Himalaya regions—and is mentioned by the Persian physician, Alheroi, in the tenth century, also by many early Arabian writers on medicine. Isa Ben Ali pronounced it to be the most rapid of deadly poisons, and describes the symptoms with tolerable correctness. The chief symptoms of poisoning by aconite are heat, numbness and tingling in the mouth and throat, giddiness, and loss of muscular power. The pupils become dilated, the skin cold, and pulse feeble, with oppressed breathing, and dread of approaching death. Finally, numbness and paralysis come on, rapidly followed by death in a few sudden gasps. The poison being extremely rapid in effect, immediate action is absolutely necessary in order to save life.

Several species of aconite grow plentifully in India, where it has been used for centuries. It is found growing at an elevation of 10,000 feet above the level of the sea, and among other places in the Singalilas, a mountain range which forms the watershed boundary between Nepal and British territory, northwest of Darjiling. *Aconitum palmatum* is collected in abundance at Tongloo, the southern termination of the Singalilas; but *A. napellus*, which is more poisonous, requires a higher elevation in which to thrive. The natives, especially the hill tribes, take aconite in the crude state as a remedy for various ailments, and every Bhotiah has a few dried roots put away in some secure corner of his hut. The method of collecting is thus described. "Early in October, when the aconite root has matured, one of the leading men of the village organises a party composed of both sexes. He, for the time, becomes their leader, settles all disputes and quarrels while out in camp, and, while keeping an account of the general expenses, supplies to each, all necessaries in the way of food. Before starting, he has to obtain a 'permit' from the Forest Department, the charge for which is 15 rupees. Carefully wrapping the pass up in a rag, and placing it in his network bag of valuables, he collects his band together, and they set out for the higher ranges. As soon as they arrive at the slopes, where aconite is growing plentifully, they at once set to work to build bamboo huts about five feet high, roofing them with leaves. After the morning meal they all set off for the lower slopes, each with basket and spade over his shoulder. But before the actual work is commenced, a ceremony has to be performed. The Bhotiahs, like the Nepalese, have a belief that the presiding demon of the hills imprisons evil spirits in the aconite plant, which fly out as soon as it is dug up and inflict dire calamity on the digger. In order, therefore, to counteract this, every morning, before the digging commences, the lama or headman, standing on a convenient hill with his followers around him, makes a fire and burns some *dhuna*, a native resin, then, inserting two fingers in his mouth, blows several shrill whistles. All wait in breathless silence till an answering whistle is heard, which may be an echo or the cry of some bird. Whatever it may be, it is taken as the dying dirge of the evil spirits, and digging begins at once.

"The roots, after being shaken from the soil, are placed in the baskets, which on return to the encampment are emptied and formed into heaps, and covered with bamboo leaves to protect them from the frost. During the day they are spread out in the sun to dry. When a sufficient quantity has been collected and dried thus, bamboo frames are fixed up with a fire below, on which the aconite is placed when the flame has died out. The one who looks after this drying process has a cloth tied round his head covering the nose, as the constant inhalation of the fumes causes a feeling of heaviness and dizziness in the head. This process is carried on three or four days until the roots are dried. When sufficient have been collected and dried, they are packed in baskets. These are shouldered, and with their cooking utensils and blankets on the top, the whole band set their faces homeward. On arrival at the commercial centre at the termination of their march the results of the expedition are soon sold, and each man is handed his share of the profits, according to the amount of aconite he has collected."

CHAPTER XI

THE only case on record in which the active principle of aconite has been used for the purpose of criminal poisoning is that of Dr. Lamson, who suffered the extreme penalty of the law for administering the drug to Percy Malcolm John, and thereby causing his death. The story is remarkable for the cold-blooded way in which the murder was carried out. George Henry Lamson, a surgeon, in impecunious circumstances, had a reversionary interest through his wife in a sum of £1,500, which would come to him on the death of his brother-in-law, Percy Malcolm John. The latter, a sickly youth of eighteen years of age, was paralysed in his lower limbs from old-standing spinal disease. On November 27, 1881, Lamson purchased two grains of aconitine, and shortly afterwards went down to the school where the lad had been placed as a boarder, and had an interview with him in the presence of the headmaster, professing at the same time a kindly interest in the lad and his health. During the interview he produced some gelatine capsules, one of which he filled with a white powder, presumed to be sugar, and directly after seeing his brother-in-law swallow it, he took his departure. Within a quarter of an hour John became unwell, saying he felt the same as when Lamson had given him a quinine pill on a former occasion. Violent vomiting soon set in, and he became unable to swallow. This was rapidly followed by delirium, and in three hours and three-quarters death ensued. Suspicion fell on Lamson, and he was arrested shortly afterwards, and charged with the murder of John.

According to evidence at the trial, it is probable that Lamson had made several previous attempts on the lad's life, with aconitine, in the form of pills and powders, which he had given him under the pretence of prescribing for his ailments. The money to which he was entitled on the death of John doubtless supplied the motive for the crime. The proof of the purchase of aconitine by the prisoner, and the evidence of the post-mortem examination, pointed to the cause of death, and the presence of aconitine was amply proved by the clinical and other tests patiently and carefully applied by the analyst. The difficulty of proving the presence of a rare vegetable alkaloid in the body after death was, no doubt, duly considered by Lamson when he fixed on aconitine as the medium for his evil design; but science proved the master of the criminal, and the evidence of the instrument by which the crime was committed was indisputably proved.

CHAPTER XII

ANTIMONY, like arsenic, to which in many ways it is closely <u>allied</u>, claims also to be ranked among the historic poisons. It was known and used by the ancient Greek and Roman physicians as a medicinal agent, and for certain purposes it is, perhaps, unequalled at the present time. The metal is a brittle, silvery and very brilliant substance, in the form of plates and crystals, and is largely used in the arts as an alloy, the most common form being Britannia metal, which is a compound of antimony, lead, and tin. The old *Poculo emetica* or everlasting emetic cups, were made of antimony. It is found abundantly in nature as a sulphide, also combined with various metals, and with quartz and limestone. From these it is separated by fusion, the heavy metallic portion sinking by the law of gravity, and abandoning the impurities which remain on the surface of the molten mass. Arsenic is a frequent contamination of commercial antimony, and it is very important that it should be eliminated before antimony is prepared for use in medicine.

Poisoning by tartarated antimony causes a peculiar metallic taste in the mouth, which is speedily followed by vomiting, burning heat, pains in the stomach and purging, difficulty in swallowing, thirst, cramp, cold perspirations, and great debility. In smaller doses it produces these effects in a mitigated form, which causes symptoms somewhat similar to natural disease, such as distaste for food, nausea, and loss of muscular power. For this reason, doubtless, it has been a favourite medium with many criminal poisoners, including Dove, Smethurst, Pritchard, and others; but there is no trial in which antimony has figured that caused more interest than the "Bravo Mystery" of 1876.

The story of this case begins with the marriage of Mr. Bravo, a young barrister of about thirty years of age, to Mrs. Ricardo, who was then a wealthy widow and a lady of considerable personal attractions. After the marriage, which followed a very short acquaintance, the couple went to reside at Balham. According to a statement made by Mrs. Bravo, she informed her husband before the marriage of a former lover, and there is little doubt that it rankled in Mr. Bravo's mind, and he frequently taunted his wife with the fact. He was a strong, healthy, and temperate man, but appears to have been both weak and vain in character. On Tuesday, April 18, 1876, after breakfast at his own house at Balham, he drove with his wife into town. On their way, a very unpleasant discussion took place. Arriving in town, he had a Turkish bath, lunched with a relative of his wife at St. James's Restaurant, and walked on his way home to Victoria Station with a friend and fellow-barrister, whom he asked out for the following day. He arrived back home about half-past four. Shortly after his return, Mr. Bravo went out for a ride, in the course of which his horse bolted and carried him a long distance, and he got back to his home very tired and exhausted. At half-past six he was noticed leaning forward on his chair, looking ill, and with his head hanging down. He ordered a hot bath, and when getting into it he cried out aloud with pain, putting his hand to his side. The bath did not appear to relieve him much, and he seemed to be suffering pain all through dinner, but appeared to avoid attracting the attention of his wife and Mrs. Cox, her companion, who dined with him.

The food provided during the dinner was partaken of more or less in common by all three, but this was not the case as regards the wine. Mr. Bravo drank Burgundy, only, while Mrs. Bravo and Mrs. Cox drank sherry and Marsala. The wine drunk by Mr. Bravo had been decanted by the butler some time before dinner; how long he could not say, but he noticed nothing unusual with it.

The wine was of good quality, and Mr. Bravo, who was something of a connoisseur of wine, remarked nothing peculiar in its taste, but drank it as usual. If he had Burgundy for luncheon he finished the bottle at dinner; but if not, as on the day in question, the remains of the bottle were put away in an unlocked cellaret in the dining-room. The butler could not remember whether any Burgundy was left on this day or not; but, however, none was discovered.

This cellaret was opened at least twice subsequently to this, and prior to Mr. Bravo's illness, once by Mrs. Cox, and once by the maid.

Mr. Bravo seems to have eaten a good dinner, although he was evidently not himself from some cause or other. It was said he was suffering from toothache or neuralgia, and had just received a letter that had given him some annoyance.

The dinner lasted till past eight o'clock, after which the party adjourned to the morning-room, where conversation continued up to about nine o'clock.

Mrs. Bravo and Mrs. Cox then retired upstairs, leaving Mr. Bravo alone, and Mrs. Cox went to fetch Mrs. Bravo some wine and water from the dining-room.

Mrs. Bravo remained in her room and prepared for bed, and drank the wine and water brought to her by Mrs. Cox, who remained with her.

The housemaid, on taking some hot water to the ladies' room, as was her usual custom at half-past nine, was asked by Mrs. Bravo to bring her some more Marsala in the glass that had contained the wine and water. On her way downstairs to the dining-room, the girl met her master at the foot of the stairs. He looked "queer" and very strange in the face, but did not appear to be in pain, according to her statement. He looked twice at her, yet did not speak, though it was his custom, but passed on.

Mr. Bravo was alone after the departure of his wife and Mrs. Cox, until the time when he passed the housemaid at the foot of the stairs. He entered his wife's dressing-room, and the maid Mrs. Bravo's bedroom. In the dressing-room, according to Mrs. Cox's statement, Mr. Bravo spoke to his wife in French, with reference to the wine. This had frequently been the subject of unpleasant remarks before; but Mrs. Bravo had no recollection of the conversation on this occasion.

After leaving his wife in her room, Mr. Bravo went to his own bedroom and closed the door. The maid left Mrs. Bravo's bedroom and met her mistress in the passage partially undressed and on her way to bed. Mrs. Bravo and Mrs. Cox entered their bedrooms, and the former drank her Marsala and went to bed.

In about a quarter of an hour Mr. Bravo's bedroom door was heard to open, and he shouted out, "Florence! Florence! Hot water." The maid ran into Mrs. Bravo's room, calling out that Mr. Bravo was ill. Mrs. Cox, who had not yet undressed, rose hastily and ran to his room. She found him standing in his night-gown at the open window, apparently vomiting, and this the maid also saw. Mrs. Cox further stated that Mr. Bravo said to her, "I have taken poison. Don't tell Florence" (alluding to his wife); and to this confession of having taken poison on the part of Mr. Bravo, Mrs. Cox adhered. After this, Mr. Bravo was again very sick, and some hot water was brought by the maid. After the vomiting he sank on the floor and became insensible, and remained so for some hours. Mrs. Cox tried to raise him, and got some mustard and water, but he could not swallow it. She then applied mustard to his feet, and coffee was procured, but he was also unable to swallow that. Meanwhile a doctor, who had attended Mrs. Bravo, and who lived at some distance, was sent for. Mrs. Bravo, who was aroused from sleep by the maid, and who seems to have been greatly excited, insisted on a nearer practitioner being sent for, and in a short time a medical man, living close by, arrived on the scene. The doctor found Mr. Bravo sitting or lying on a chair, completely unconscious, and the heart's action almost suspended. He had him laid on the bed, and then administered some hot brandy and water, but was unable to get him to swallow it. In about half an hour another medical man arrived, and was met by Mrs. Cox, who said she was sure Mr. Bravo had taken chloroform. Both doctors came to the conclusion that the patient was in a dangerous state, and endeavoured to administer restoratives. Realizing the critical nature of the case, Dr. George Johnson, of King's College Hospital, was sent for. Meanwhile, Mr. Bravo was again seized with vomiting, mostly blood, and the doctors came to the conclusion he was suffering from some irritant poison. About three o'clock he became conscious and able to be questioned. He was at once asked, "What have you taken?" But from first to last he persisted in declaring, in the most solemn manner, that he had taken nothing except some laudanum for toothache. In reply to other questions, asking him if there were any poisons about the house, he replied there was only the laudanum and chloroform for toothache, some Condy's Fluid, and "rat poison in the stable." Mr. Bravo did not lose consciousness again until the time of his death, which occurred fifty-five and a half hours after he was first taken ill.

At an early period his bedroom was searched, but nothing was found but the laudanum bottle, and a little chloroform and camphor liniment which had been brought from another room. There were no remains of any solid poison in paper, glass, or tumbler, and nothing to indicate any poison had been taken. The post-mortem examination showed evidence of great gastric irritation, extending downwards, but there was no appearance of any disease in the body, or inflammation, congestion, or ulceration. It was left therefore to the chemical examination to show what was the irritating substance which had been introduced into the body, and supply a key to part of the mystery. The matters which had been vomited in the early stage of Mr. Bravo's illness had been thrown away; but, singular to relate, on examination of the leads of the house beneath the bedroom window, some portion of the matter was found undisturbed, although much rain had fallen and the greater part must have been washed away. This was carefully collected and handed to Professor Redwood for analysis. From this matter he extracted a large amount of antimony. Antimony was also discovered in the liver and other parts of the body, and it was concluded that altogether nearly forty grains of this poison must have been swallowed by the unfortunate man. How he came to swallow this enormous dose, whether the design was homicidal or suicidal, there was not the slightest evidence to show, or where the antimony was obtained. The whole affair was shrouded in mystery, and a mystery it remains.

CHAPTER XIII

THE CASE OF DR. PRITCHARD

THE remarkable case of Dr. E. W. Pritchard of Glasgow, who was arrested and charged with murdering his wife and mother-in-law in that city in the year 1865, excited great interest at the time. The respectable position occupied by the accused man in society in Glasgow, and the practice as a physician which he had been enabled to attain in the course of his six years' residence there, awakened an unusual degree of attention in the public mind when the fact of his apprehension became known. The excitement was strengthened by the mystery invariably attached to the prosecution of all criminal inquiries in Scotland.

It appears that for some time previous to her decease, Mrs. Pritchard had been in a delicate state of heath, and her mother, Mrs Taylor, wife of Mr. Taylor, a silk weaver of Edinburgh, had gone to Glasgow to nurse her during her illness. Mrs. Taylor took up her abode in the house of Dr. Pritchard, and ministered to her daughter's comfort; but while so engaged she became ill, and died suddenly, about three weeks previous to the day on which the accused man was apprehended. The cause of death was assigned to apoplexy, and as Mrs. Taylor was about seventy years of age no public attention was awakened, and the body was conveyed to Edinburgh and buried in the Grange Cemetery.

Circumstances closely following on this, however, awakened grave suspicions. Mrs. Pritchard died shortly after her mother, and a report was circulated that she had succumbed to gastric fever. The family grave at the Grange was fixed on as the place of interment, and arrangements were made for the funeral without delay. The body was taken to Edinburgh by rail, and Dr. Pritchard accompanied it to the house of his father-in-law, where it was to await interment. The deaths of the two ladies occurring within so short an interval of each other, coupled with certain hints which they had received, set the police on the alert, and while Dr. Pritchard was absent in Edinburgh they instituted inquiries, which led to a warrant being issued for his apprehension. On his return to Glasgow, previous to the day fixed for the funeral, he was arrested at the railway station in Queen Street and conveyed to the police offices.

Meanwhile the authorities had transmitted to Edinburgh information of what had been done, and at the same time had issued a warrant for a post-mortem examination of the body of Mrs. Pritchard. This was entrusted to Professor Douglas Maclagan, assisted by Drs. Arthur Gamgee and Littlejohn. The result of the post-mortem proved that death had not resulted from natural causes, and a subsequent examination disclosed the presence of minute particles of antimony in the liver.

The case now assumed a grave and mysterious aspect, and the authorities resolved to carry the investigations further. The next step was to order the exhumation of the body of Mrs. Taylor. This having been effected, the internal organs were submitted to analysis by Professor Maclagan, Dr. Littlejohn, and Professor Penny of Glasgow, who, after a protracted examination, reported that the death of Mrs. Taylor, like that of her daughter, was due to poisoning by antimony. On these facts being elicited, Dr. Pritchard was fully committed on the charge of murdering Jane Taylor his mother-in- law and Mary Jane Pritchard his wife.

The trial opened on July 3, 1865, at the High Court of Justiciary, Edinburgh, before the Lord Justice-Clerk, Lord Ardmillan, and Lord Jervis-woode, the Solicitor-General prosecuting for the Crown, while the prisoner was defended by Messrs. A. R. Clark, Watson, and Brand.

Evidence was given that Mrs. Pritchard was first taken ill in the October of 1864, with constant vomiting, often accompanied by severe cramp.

After being treated by her husband for some time, and getting no better, at her own request a Dr. Gairdner was called in, and her mother, Mrs. Taylor, came from Edinburgh to nurse her.

While on this visit to her daughter, Mrs. Taylor, on February 24, complained of feeling unwell. The next day she was found insensible, sitting on her chair in her daughter's room, and died the same night. From this time Mrs. Pritchard got gradually worse, and died within three weeks afterwards.

Mary McLeod, a girl who had been in the service of the prisoner, admitted that he had familiar relations with her, and that this fact was known to Mrs. Pritchard.

The doctor had also made her presents, and told her he would marry her if his wife died.

Dr. Paterson, a medical practitioner of Glasgow, who was called in to see Mrs. Taylor, stated Pritchard told him the old lady was in the habit of taking Batley's solution of opium, and a few days before her death, she had purchased a half-pound bottle. When he saw her, he was convinced her symptoms betokened that she was under the depressing influence of antimony, and not opium. He therefore refused to give a certificate of her death.

Pritchard eventually signed the certificate himself, stating the primary cause of death had been paralysis and the secondary cause apoplexy. He further certified Mrs. Pritchard's death as due to gastric fever.

It was proved on the evidence of two chemists, that Pritchard was in the habit of purchasing tartarated antimony in large quantities, and also Fleming's tincture of aconite.

Dr. Maclagan, professor of medical jurisprudence in the University of Edinburgh, was then called to give the result of the chemical examination of the various organs of the body of Mrs. Pritchard, which had been retained for analysis. Antimony, corresponding to one-fourth of a grain of tartar emetic, was found in the urine, in small quantities in the bile and blood, and as much as four grains in the whole liver. Evidence of the presence of antimony was also found in the spleen, kidney, muscular substance of the heart, coats of the stomach and rectum, the brain and uterus.

Antimony was also detected in various stains on linen and articles of clothing, which had been worn by Mrs. Pritchard during her illness.

From these results Dr. Maclagan concluded that Mrs. Pritchard had taken a large quantity of antimony in the form of tartar emetic, which caused her death, and that from the extent to which the whole organs and fluids of the body were impregnated with the drug, it must have been given in repeated doses up to within a few hours of her decease.

The result of the chemical examination of the various organs of the body of Mrs. Taylor, which was exhumed for this purpose, revealed the presence of ·279, or a little more than a quarter of a grain of antimony in the contents of the stomach. Antimony was also found in the blood, and 1·151 grain was recovered from 1,000 grains of the liver.

Dr. Penny, who made an independent analysis, found distinct evidence of antimony in the liver, spleen, kidney, brain, heart, blood, and rectum, but no trace of morphine or aconite. He also came to the conclusion that Mrs Pritchard's death had resulted from the effects of antimony.

Antimony was found mixed with tapioca contained in a packet discovered in the house, also in a bottle containing Batley's solution of opium found in the prisoner's surgery.

Dr. Littlejohn, surgeon to the Edinburgh police, who was present at the post-mortem examination of both women, gave his opinion that Mrs. Pritchard's death had been due to the administration of antimony in small quantities, and that continuously. In Mrs. Taylor's case he believed some strong narcotic poison had been administered with the antimony.

This opinion was further endorsed by Dr. Paterson. Evidence was offered, that

Pritchard had been in the habit of purchasing large quantities of Batley's solution of opium, which the manufacturers swore contained no antimony. For the defence it was urged, that there was no proof whatever that poison had had been administered by the prisoner, who had always lived on affectionate terms with his wife, and that the motive suggested was of the most trifling nature; that the stronger suspicion pointed to the maidservant Mary McLeod, on whose uncorroborated statements the chief evidence against the prisoner lay. The senior counsel for the prisoner (Mr. Clark) concluded his address by stating that the Crown had admitted there were but two persons who could have committed the crime—the prisoner, and Mary M'Leod. Mary M'Leod's hand had been found in connexion with every one of the acts in which poison was said to have been administered in the food. The case against the prisoner seemed to depend on a series of suspicions and probabilities, and not upon legal proof; and upon these grounds he asked a verdict of acquittal.

The "summing up" of the Lord Justice-Clerk occupied three hours and twenty minutes, on the conclusion of which the jury retired to consider their verdict. After an absence of fifty-five minutes they returned with the following verdict —"The jury unanimously find the prisoner guilty of both charges as libelled."

Dr. Pritchard was thereupon sentenced to death, and was executed at Glasgow on July 28, 1865.

There can be no doubt that he fully deserved his terrible doom.

CHAPTER XIV

THE PIMLICO MYSTERY

Chloroform belongs to the class of neurotic poisons which act on the brain, and produce loss of sensation. It is a colourless, heavy, and volatile liquid, having a peculiar ethereal odour which cannot be easily mistaken, and a sweet pungent taste when diluted. For producing insensibility it requires very careful and experienced administration, and more lives have been lost by carelessness in using, than from the noxious character of the drug.

Many stories are related of the peculiar hallucinations and remarks made by patients while under, or partially under the influence of chloroform. The following has the merit of being true:—

"Doctor (*who has just administered chloroform to a lady*): 'Nurse, some 1 in 1,000, if you please.'

"Patient (*under the anæsthetic*): 'Ah! that's my Jack. He's one in a thousand. Dear Jack!'"

The stories that crop up from time to time, of persons who have been rendered unconscious by simply waving a chloroformed handkerchief before the face, usually emanate from the fertile brain of some imaginative journalist. As an internal poison chloroform has rarely been used, although there are many cases on record where persons have accustomed themselves to drinking chloroform, until they have been able to swallow it in very large quantities. The one recorded instance in which it was alleged to have been used for the criminal destruction of life was in the remarkable case known as the "Pimlico Mystery."

The trial of Adelaide Bartlett for the wilful murder of her husband by administering chloroform to him, was held before Mr. Justice Wills at the Central Criminal Court on April 12, 1886, and lasted for six days. The case attracted considerable attention and interest throughout, which culminated in a dramatic scene at the close, and the acquittal of the accused woman. The strange relations which existed between Mrs. Bartlett and her husband, with whose murder she was charged, the yet more strange relations between her and the man who in the first instance was included in the accusation, together with the exceptional circumstances of his acquittal, and his immediate appearance in the witness box formed a case of peculiar dramatic interest. Thomas Edwin Bartlett was a grocer, having several shops in the suburbs of London, and at the time of his death was forty years of age. In 1875 he married a Frenchwoman, Adelaide Blanche de la Tremoille, who was a native of Orleans, and whom he met at the house of his brother, she being at that time about twenty years of age. After the marriage she went to a boarding- school at Stoke Newington, and lived with her husband only during the vacation. At a later period she went to a convent school in Belgium, where she remained for some eighteen months, after which she rejoined her husband, and settled down to live in London. During Christmas of 1881 she gave birth to a stillborn child, which so affected her that she came to the resolution that she would have no more children. Some four years later Bartlett and his wife made the acquaintance of George Dyson, a young Wesleyan minister, who soon became on terms of great social intimacy with them, visiting and dining with them frequently. The admiration for their friend seems to have been common to both husband and wife. In 1885 Edwin Bartlett made a will, leaving all he possessed to his wife, and making Mr. Dyson and his solicitors his executors. Shortly afterwards the couple removed to furnished apartments in Claverton Street, Pimlico, where they apparently lived on good terms, and were still frequently visited by their friend Mr. Dyson.

On December 10, in the same year, Mr. Bartlett became seriously ill. Peculiar symptoms developed, which excited the curiosity and surprise of the medical man called in to attend him. The state of his gums suggested to the doctor that the illness was due to mercury, which in some way was being taken or administered to him, and he complained of nervous depression and sleeplessness. He appeared to be gradually recovering from this, but on December 19, Mr. Bartlett himself suggested that a second doctor should be called in, lest, as he put it, "his friends should suspect, if anything happened to him, that his wife was poisoning him." The cause for this was put down to some ill-feeling which had formerly existed between Mrs. Bartlett and her husband's father. A second practitioner, therefore, was called in, and the patient, on December 26, was practically well and went out for a drive though still weak.

The next day Mrs. Bartlett asked Mr. Dyson, who was constantly calling at the house, to procure for her a considerable quantity of chloroform, which she told him she had used before with good effect on her husband for some internal ailment of long standing, and that this internal affliction had upon previous occasions given him paroxysms. She further expressed apparently some belief that he might die suddenly in one of these attacks. Dyson seems meekly to have yielded to her request, and obtained three different lots of chloroform, in all six ounces, from various chemists, giving the reason, that he required it for taking out grease spots, and placed it all together in one bottle. Two days after he met Mrs. Bartlett on the Embankment and handed her the chloroform. During his illness, Mr. Bartlett had slept on a camp bedstead in the front drawing-room, his wife occupying a sofa in the same room. On December 31 he was apparently quite well again, and about half-past ten o'clock in the evening, Mrs. Bartlett told the servant she required nothing else and retired with her husband for the night. At four o'clock in the morning the house was aroused by Mrs. Bartlett, and it was discovered her husband was dead in bed.

The statement made by the lady was, that when her husband had settled for the night she sat down at the foot of the bed; that her hand was resting upon his feet; that she dozed off in her chair; she awoke with a sensation of cramp, and was horrified to find her husband's feet were deathly cold. She tried to pour some brandy down his throat, and she found he was dead. She then aroused the household. The first person who entered the room was the landlord, who noticed a peculiar smell that reminded him of chloric ether. The doctor was promptly sent for, but from external examination could find nothing to account for death. The only bottle found was one that contained a drop or two of chlorodyne. A post-mortem examination was held, and the stomach showed evidence of having contained a considerable quantity of chloroform. There was no internal disease or growth, the organs being quite healthy, and nothing to account for death beyond the chloroform, which the medical men concluded must have been the cause of death.

The coroner's inquiry resulted in a verdict of wilful murder against Adelaide Bartlett and George Dyson, and they were both arrested. At the trial, the Crown decided to offer no evidence against Dyson, and, after being indicted and pleading "Not guilty," he was discharged by the judge to be called as a witness.

A brilliant array of counsel were engaged on the case, the late Lord Chief Justice, then Sir Charles Russell, having charge of the prosecution, while the defence of Mrs. Bartlett was entrusted to Sir Edward Clark, and that of Mr. Dyson to Mr. Lockwood.

Dyson's examination occupied nearly the whole of the second day, during which he detailed the form of the intimacy between Mrs. Bartlett and himself; how he procured the chloroform and disposed of the bottles after hearing the result of the post-mortem, by throwing them away on Wandsworth Common while on his way to preach at Tooting. He was in the habit of kissing Mrs. Bartlett, and usually called her Adelaide. He had had conversations with Mr. Bartlett on the subject of marriage, and had heard him express the opinion that a man should have two wives, one to look after the household duties, and another to be a companion and confidante. He had told Mr. Bartlett he was becoming attached to his wife, but the latter seemed to encourage it, and asked him to continue the intimacy. He did not mention the matter of having procured the chloroform for Mrs. Bartlett until he had heard the result of the post-mortem.

The medical man called in to attend Mr. Bartlett during his illness, described the condition in which he found him, and his recovery from the illness. He also gave an account of a very extraordinary statement, which was made to him by Mrs. Bartlett after the death of her husband. It was as follows. At the age of sixteen years she was selected by Mr. Bartlett as a wife for companionship only, and for whom no carnal feeling should be entertained. The marriage compact was, that they should live together simply as loving friends. This rule was faithfully observed for about six years of their married life, and then only broken at her earnest and repeated entreaty that she should be permitted to be really a wife and a mother. The child was still-born, and from that time the two lived together, but their relations were not those of matrimony. Her husband showed great affection for her of an ultra-platonic kind, and encouraged her to pursue studies of various kinds, which she did to please him. He affected to admire her, and liked to surround her with male acquaintances, and enjoy their attentions to her. Then they became acquainted with Dyson. Her husband conceived a great liking for him, and threw them together. He requested them to kiss in his presence and seemed to enjoy it, and gave her to understand that he had "given her" to Mr. Dyson. As her husband gradually recovered from his illness he expressed a wish that they should resume the ordinary relations of man and wife, but she resented it. She therefore sought for some means to prevent his desire, and for this purpose she asked Dyson to procure the chloroform.

On the night of the death, some conversation of this kind had taken place between them, and when he was in bed she brought the bottle of chloroform and gave it to him, informing him of her intention to sprinkle some upon a handkerchief and wave it in his face, thinking that thereby he would go peacefully to sleep. He looked at the bottle and placed it by the side of the low bed, then turning over on his side apparently went to sleep. She fell asleep also, sitting at the foot of the bed, with her arm round his foot; she heard him snoring, then woke again, and found he was dead.

Dr. Stevenson, who made the analysis, gave evidence as to finding eleven and a quarter grains of pure chloroform in the stomach of the deceased, but, judging from the time that had elapsed and the very volatile nature of the liquid, a large quantity must have been swallowed. No other poisons were found. The jury, after deliberating nearly two hours, returned a verdict of "Not guilty," thus making another addition to the list of unsolved poisoning mysteries.

CHAPTER XV

STRYCHNINE may very justly be termed a deadly poison. It is one of the active principles extracted from nux vomica, the singular disk-like seed of the *Strychnos nux vomica*, a tree indigenous to most parts of India, Burmah, Northern Australia, and other countries. Nux vomica was unknown to the ancients, and is said to have been introduced into medicine by the Arabians, but there is very little reliable record of it until the seventeenth century, when the seeds were used for poisoning animals and birds. Strychnine was discovered in 1818 by Pelletier and Carenton, and was first extracted from St. Ignatius' bean, in which it is present to the extent of about 1·5 per cent. Very soon afterwards it was extracted from nux vomica, which, being very plentiful, is now the chief source of the drug. It is extremely bitter in taste, and may be distinctly detected in a solution containing no more than one-six- hundred-thousandth part. For a considerable time after its discovery, the detection of strychnine in the body after death was a matter of great uncertainty, especially when only a small quantity had been administered; but now it is possible to detect the presence of one-five-thousandth part of a grain, and that even after some period has elapsed. It has been used for criminal purposes by several notorious poisoners, notably by Dove, Palmer, and Cream, but the symptoms produced are so marked and its presence clearly indicated, that detection now is almost certain.

Among the most celebrated trials of this century was that of Dr. Palmer, who was charged with the wilful murder of John Parscns Cook, at Rugeley, in 1855. A special Act of Parliament was passed in order to have this case tried in London, where it was brought before Lord Chief Justice Campbell, Mr. Baron Alderson, and Mr. Justice Cresswell, at the Central Criminal Court, on May 14, 1856. The Attorney General, Mr. E. James, Q.C., with several other counsel, conducted the prosecution, and Palmer was defended by Mr. Serjeant Shee, Messrs. Grove, Q.C., Gray, and Kenealy.

The accused man was a country doctor, and had carried on a medical practice in Rugeley, a small town in Staffordshire, for some years. Then he went on the turf, and made his business over to a man named Thirlby, a former assistant. Shortly afterwards, he made the acquaintance of John P. Cook over some betting transactions. Cook was a young man of good family, about twenty-eight years of age, and was intended for the legal profession. He was articled to a solicitor; but after a time, inheriting some property worth between twelve and fifteen thousand pounds, he abandoned law and commenced to keep racehorses. Meeting Palmer at various race meetings, they soon became very intimate. In a very short time Palmer got into difficulties, and was compelled to raise money on bills. Things went from bad to worse—until he at last forged an acceptance to a bill in his mother's name, who was possessed of considerable property. In 1854 he owed a large sum of money, and in the same year his wife died, whose life, it transpired, he had insured for £13,000. With this money he bought two racehorses; but in his betting transactions he lost heavily, and then commenced to borrow money from Cook, whose name he also forged on one occasion on the back of a cheque. He insured his brother's life for £13,000, and very shortly after *he* died, the amount being also paid to Palmer. This money soon went, and at length he had two writs out against him for £4,000.

In the meanwhile, Cook had been more successful than his friend in his racing ventures, and had won a considerable amount with a race-horse he owned called Polestar. Polestar was entered for the Shrewsbury races on November 14, 1855, and Cook and Palmer went there and stayed with some friends at the same hotel in that town. On the evening of the races they were drinking brandy and water together. Cook asked Palmer to have some more, and the latter replied, "Not unless you finish your glass." Cook, noticing he had some still left in his tumbler, said, "I'll soon do that," and finished it at a draught. On swallowing it he immediately exclaimed, "There's something in it burns my throat." Palmer took up the glass and said, "Nonsense, there is nothing in it," and called the attention of the others standing by. Cook then suddenly left the room, and was seized with violent vomiting. This became so bad that he soon had to be taken to bed, and appeared to be very seriously ill. Two hours later a medical man was sent for, who at once prescribed an emetic, and then a pill. He obtained relief from these, and by the morning the vomiting had ceased, and he was much better, though he still felt very unwell. They returned to Rugeley together, Cook taking rooms at an hotel directly opposite Palmer's house. Cook was still confined to his room, and during the next few days, was constantly visited by Palmer, and after each visit it was noticed the sickness commenced again. On one occasion Palmer had some broth prepared, which he specially wished Cook to take. The latter tried to swallow it, but was immediately sick. It was then taken downstairs, and a woman at the hotel, thinking it looked nice, took a couple of tablespoonfuls of it; but within half an hour she was taken seriously ill, and obliged to go to bed, her symptoms being exactly like those of Cook's when first taken ill at Shrewsbury. Three days after this a neighbouring doctor was called in, Palmer telling him that Cook was suffering from a bilious attack. Palmer then suddenly went off to London, his business being to try and arrange about the settlement of some debts that were pressing. From the time he left, it was noticed by the doctor that Cook's condition rapidly improved, and in a day or two he was able to leave his bed and be up and dressed. On Palmer's return to Rugeley he at once went to see Cook and during the rest of his illness was constantly with him. On the evening of his return he also called on a surgeon's assistant, with whom he was acquainted, and purchased from him three grains of strychnine. Cook was taking some pills which had been prescribed by the doctor, and which had done him good. They were ordered to be taken at bedtime, and the box containing them was in his room. He was visited by Palmer about 11 o'clock the same night, and up to that time he was apparently well. Palmer left shortly after. At 12 o'clock the whole house was aroused by violent screams proceeding from Cook's room. The servants rushed in and found him writhing in great agony, shouting "Murder!" He was evidently suffering intense pain, and soon was seized with convulsions. Palmer was at once sent for, and on his arrival Cook was gasping for breath, and hardly able to speak. He ran back to procure some medicine, which on his return he gave him, but the sick man at once threw it back. The attack gradually passed off, and by the morning he was somewhat better, but very weak. The same day Palmer visited a chemist he knew in the town, and purchased six grains of strychnine. During the afternoon a relative of Palmer's, who was also a medical man, arrived on a visit to Rugeley, and he was taken to see Cook, and in the evening a consultation was held by the three medical men. They agreed to prescribe some medicine for the patient in the form of pills, which were prepared, and in the course of the evening were handed to Palmer, who was to administer a dose the last thing at night.

About half-past ten Palmer gave Cook two of the pills, settled him comfortably for the night, and went home. At ten minutes to eleven Cook roused the house with a frightful scream, calling out, "I'm going to be ill as I was last night." Palmer was sent for, and brought with him two more pills, which he said contained ammonia, and gave them to Cook. Very shortly afterwards convulsions set in, which were followed by tetanus, and the unfortunate man died in a few minutes in great agony.

The deceased man's relatives were communicated with, and his father-in-law soon arrived in Rugeley. On Palmer being questioned about Cook's affairs, he said that he held a paper drawn up by a lawyer, and signed by Cook, stating that, in respect of £4,000 worth of bills, he (Cook) was alone liable, and Palmer had a claim for that amount against the estate. This, with other matters, aroused suspicion, and it was decided to hold a post-mortem examination on the body to ascertain the cause of death. Palmer was present at the examination, and by his deliberate act the fluid contents of the stomach were lost. What portions of the body were reserved for analysis, he did all he could to prevent from reaching the analysts. When the jars, etc. were being sent to London for examination by the Government analyst, he intercepted them, and offered the post-boy £10 to upset the conveyance and break them.

The evidence offered at the trial was almost entirely circumstantial, and the medical testimony was very conflicting. It was supposed, in the first instance, Palmer had administered tartar emetic to his victim, but that for the fatal dose strychnine was used. It was proved Palmer had purchased strychnine under suspicious circumstances on the morning of the day on which Cook died, and could not account for the purchase of it, or state what he had done with it. The symptoms appeared at a time which would correspond to the interval that precedes the action of strychnine, being developed over the entire body and limbs in a few minutes, suddenly and with violence. None of the pills could be obtained for analysis, and Dr. Taylor, who made the analytical examination, was unable to find any trace of strychnine in the portions submitted to him, but he found half a grain of antimony in the blood. He believed Cook died from the effects of strychnine. The great point in the case was, did the tetanic symptoms, under which the deceased man died, depend on disease or poison? Doctors Brodie, Christison and Todd, and other eminent authorities of the time agreed, that when taken as a whole they were not in accordance with any form of disease, but were in perfect accordance with the effects of strychnine. On the other hand, medical men called for the defence testified that tetanus might be caused by natural disease, and the deceased might have died from angina pectoris or epilepsy. In spite of the absence of confirmatory chemical evidence, after one hour and seventeen minutes' deliberation, the jury returned a verdict of "Guilty," and Palmer was sentenced to death, the trial having lasted twelve days.

The rigid and fixed condition of the limbs is a marked feature after poisoning by strychnine. In the recent Horsford case, in which a farmer named Walter Horsford was convicted of the murder of his cousin Annie Holmes, at St. Neot's, in 1897, 3·69 grains of strychnine were recovered from the internal organs, after the body was exhumed, *nineteen days* after death. Even then, rigidity was very marked, especially in the lower limbs and fingers. The same rigidity was remarked by Dr. Stevenson in the case of Matilda Clover, who was poisoned by Neill Cream with strychnine a few years ago. In this case, the body had been buried *from October until May*, and the rigidity in the limbs and fingers was still maintained. Dr. Stevenson states that usually when persons are suffering from strychnine poisoning, they are very apprehensive of death. He has known a woman say, "I am going to die" before any intimation of symptoms had occurred. The first apprehension is, that some terrible calamity is about to take place.

CHAPTER XVI

T<small>HE</small> narcotic <u>properties</u> of the poppy have been known from times of great antiquity. The first mention we have of its use is by Theophrastus, who lived about 300 years B.C. It is supposed that the potion known under the name of Nepenthe, prepared by Helen of Troy, and given to the guests of Menelaus, to drive away their care, was none other than a wine of opium. This conjecture receives support from Homer, who states that Nepenthe was obtained from Thebes, the ancient capital of Egypt. According to Prosper Alpinus, the Egyptians were practised opium eaters, and were often faint and languid through the want of it. They prepared and drank it in the form of "Cretic Wine," which they flavoured and made hotter by the addition of pepper and other aromatics. The Turks and Persians employed opium as a medicine, and also for eating, from a very early period. Dioscorides, the ancient Greek pharmacist, describes how the capsules from which the drug is collected should be cut, and Celsus, a Roman physician of the first century, frequently alludes to opium in his works under the quaint name of "poppy tears."

The introduction of opium into India seems to have been connected with the spread of Mahomedanism, the earliest record we have of its use in that country being made by Barbosa in 1511, although it is more than probable it was used in India long before that time. Pyres, the first ambassador from Europe to China in 1516, speaks of the opium of Egypt, Cambay, and the kingdom of Coûs, in Bengal, and states it was eaten by "the kings and lords, and even the common people, though not so much because it costs dear." The Mogul Government uniformly sold the opium monopoly, and the East India Company did likewise.

The properties of opium have also been known from early times to the Persians, who flavoured the drug with aromatics, and held it in great esteem. By them it was commonly called Theriaka. It is supposed to have been first introduced to China by the Arabs, who traded with the Chinese as early as the ninth century. Towards the end of the eighteenth century a trade sprang up with India, which rapidly increased, till it led to political difficulties, culminating in the war of 1842, and the signing of the treaty of Nanking, after which five ports of China were opened to foreign trade, opium being admitted as a legalised import in 1858. Opium smoking in China was practised in the seventeenth century, and gradually extended over the entire empire, and at the present time is almost a recognised habit among the people.

With regard to the introduction of opium into India, the Mahomedans once having established its use began to make it a source of income. The Great Mogul monopolized the opium production and trade, and derived an immense income from the sale of the monopoly. With respect to its use in India, it is not easy to state with certainty whether or not and in what periods, it has increased over the various parts of the country. From the most recent reports it appears that "the largest amount of opium is produced in the central tract of the Ganges, extending from Dinapore in the east, to Agra in the west, and from Gorakhpur in the north to Hazaribagh in the south, and comprising an area of about 600 miles long and 200 miles broad." In the district of Bengal, the Government has the monopoly of the opium industry, and the districts are divided into two agencies, Behar and Benares, which are under the control of officers residing in Patna and Ghazipur. In 1883 the amount of acres under poppy cultivation was in Behar 463,829, and in Benares agency 412,625; but the export of opium has somewhat diminished since then. Any one may undertake the industry, but cultivators are obliged to sell the opium exclusively to the Government agencies, at a price which is fixed beforehand by the officials. The Government sells the ready goods to merchants at a much higher price, which difference is paid by the country to which the opium is exported. In India itself, the sale of opium is restricted to licensed shopkeepers, a practice which has proved to be useful, because in some places, when the licensed shops have been closed, a greater number of unlicensed and secret shops have sprung up, and have made the contract insufficient.

The opium question is so complex in its nature, and is so largely influenced by the habits and constitution of those nations who are addicted to its use, that it is obvious that only those with skilled medical knowledge, who are on the spot and have lived and had a daily experience of the people, are in a proper position to deal with the question at all. So much has been written by religious enthusiasts, and other persons totally ignorant of the nature and properties of the drug, that one almost hesitates to touch upon the question at all. Our only excuse for so doing is, that the following facts have been furnished by reliable medical authorities, who are really in a position to judge on the subject.

The cause which led to the use of this narcotic drug by the races of the East may have been primarily due to the prohibition of wine by the Moslems, but more likely on account of its valuable remedial or protective properties, needed by a race subject to malaria and kindred diseases, and to counteract the effect of the hot climate to which they are exposed. It is a remedy at hand, and would seem to be one to which they at once fly. The evil lies more in the smoking than the eating of the drug; the former habit is more prevalent in China, and has the most demoralizing effect. The extent of its use in the East varies according to the geographical and social differences of the people, and it is used in various degrees of moderation and excess.

The drug is employed in various forms, according to the class of people who consume it. In India it is largely used in the crude state, and is sold at about two annas a drachm, in small square pieces. The opium eater will take two or three grains and roll them into the form of a pill between his fingers, and then chew or swallow it, often twenty times in the day. It is also used in a liquid form called Kusambah made by macerating opium in rose-water; others boil it with milk, then collect the cream and eat it. The varieties for smoking are known as Chundoo and Mudat, the former being a very impure extract of a fairly stiff consistence, and the latter made from the refuse of Chundoo, of which it largely consists; but being much cheaper, is chiefly used by the low-class Hindoos and Mahomedans. From two to four grains a day may be called a moderate use of the crude drug. The poorer people regularly give it to children up to two years of age, to keep them quiet, also as a preventive against such complaints as enteritis, so common in the East; and so before youth is reached they become inured to its action. Licences to sell the drug are sold to the highest bidder at the opium auctions, the licensee having the privilege of supplying a certain number of small dealers.

The Chinese smoker usually lays himself down on his side, with his head supported by a pillow. On the straw mat beside him, between his doubled-up knees and his nose, a small glass oil lamp, covered with a glass shade, is burning. Close to this is a tray, containing a small round box holding the drug, a straight piece of wire used for manipulating it, a knife to scrape up fragments, and the pipe used for smoking. The latter is about two feet long, with a bore of about half an inch in diameter, and is not unlike the stem of a flute before it is fitted. About two inches from the bottom of the tube, is a closed cup or bowl of earthenware or stone, having a central perforation. To charge the pipe, a small portion of the drug (weighing a few grains) is picked up with the wire, kneaded and rolled in the closed surface of the cup, then heated in the flame of the lamp till it swells. This is rolled up and again manipulated, then finally placed in the aperture in the surface of the bowl. It is then lighted from the lamp, and the smoke drawn into the lungs through the tube till the first charge is exhausted.

In a report made by the *British Medical Journal* concerning the use of opium in India, from the evidence of medical men long resident in that country, there seems a general concensus of opinion that opium eating, in the majority of cases, exercises no unfavourable influence on the people who indulge in the habit, and that it is a prophylactic against fever, and prevents the natives from malaria and excessive fatigue. There is no comparison between the effects of the opium habit and the habitual use of alcohol. English people cannot judge from their own standard, the manners and customs of people living under conditions with which they are unacquainted. While we look on opium as a narcotic, the Hindoo uses it as a stimulant to enable him to go through hard work on the smallest quantity possible of food. In Persia, at the present time, according to Wills, nine out of ten of the aged, take from one to five grains of the drug daily. It is largely used by the native physicians. It does not appear that the moderate use of Persian opium in the country itself, is deleterious. Opium smoking is almost unknown, and when it is smoked, it is, as a rule, by a doctor's orders. The opium pill-box—a tiny box of silver—is as common in Persia as the snuff-box was once with us. Most men of forty in the middle and upper classes use it. They take from a grain to a grain and a half, divided into two pills, one in the afternoon and one at night. The majority of authorities agree that opium smoking as a habit is much more harmful and attended with more demoralizing influences than opium eating; but either habit is undoubtedly harmful to Europeans, and when once formed, is extremely difficult to break.

Paracelsus is generally credited with being the originator of the word "laudanum," which is now employed as the popular name for tincture of opium. Yet there seems little doubt the word was first applied to the gum of the cistus. Clusius in his "Rariorum Plantarum Historia" states, "The gum of the cistus is called in Greek and Latin, ladanum, and in shops laudanum." It is therefore very likely that the secret preparation originated by Paracelsus which he called laudanum, was composed of the gum of the cistus as well as opium, and that he adopted the title from the former ingredient.

The Kiowa and other Mexican Indians use the fruit of the *Anhelonium Lewinii*, which they call "mescal buttons," to produce a species of intoxication and stimulation during certain of their religious ceremonies. The effects of this fruit, which like Indian hemp varies considerably in different individuals, are very peculiar, and have been described by Lewin, Prentiss and Morgan.

The eating of the fruit first results in a state of strange excitement and great exuberance of spirits, accompanied by great volubility in speech. This is shortly followed by a stage of intoxication in which the sight is affected in a very extraordinary manner, consisting of a kaleidoscopic play of colours ever in motion, of every possible shade and tint, and these constantly changing. The pupils of the eyes are widely dilated, cutaneous sensation is blunted, and thoughts seem to flash through the brain with extraordinary rapidity. The colour visions are generally only seen with closed eyes, but the colouring of all external objects is exaggerated. Sometimes there is also an indescribable sensation of dual existence.

Recent investigation into the pharmacology of the mescal plant prove it to be a poison of a very powerful nature. Lethal doses produce complete paralysis, and death is caused by respiratory failure.

CHAPTER XVII

H<small>ASHISH</small>, or Bhang, is the native term applied to the dried flowering tops of the Indian hemp, from which the resin has not been removed.

This plant, cultivated largely in India, is now considered to be the same, botanically, as the *Cannabis sativa* of European cultivation; but there is great difference in their medicinal activity, that growing in India being much more powerful. Ganja is the native name for part of the plant, and Sidhi for another part, which is much poorer in resin. The resinous principle is called *churrus* or *charas*, and the entire plant, cut during inflorescence, dried in the sun and pressed into bundles, is called *bhang*.

The method of using it in India is chiefly for smoking in combination with tobacco. For this purpose, a plug of tobacco is first placed at the bottom of the bowl of the pipe, on the top a small piece of hashish, and over this a piece of glowing charcoal. Another way is to knead the drug with the tobacco by the thumb of one hand working in the palm of the other, till they are thoroughly incorporated. Simple infusions of the leaves and flowering tops are also much used for drinking purposes by old and young in India, the alcoholic form being a most active and dangerous intoxicant.

The antiquity of the drug is great, and it is said to have been used in China as early as the year 220, to produce insensibility when performing operations. The Persians employed it in the Middle Ages for the purpose of exciting the pugnacity and fanaticism of the soldiers during the wars of the Crusades.

In 1803 Visey, a French scientist, published a memoir on hashish, and attempted to prove that it was the Nepenthe of Homer; there is little doubt, however, that the use of the drug was known to Galen.

Silvestin de Lacy contends that the word assassin is derived from "hashishin," a name given to a wild sect of Mahomedans who committed murder under its influence.

The Chinese herbal, Rh-ya, which dates from about the fifth century, B.C., notices the fact that the hemp plant is of two kinds, the one producing seeds and the other flowers only. Herodotus states that hemp grows in Scythia both wild and cultivated, and that the Thracians made garments from it which can hardly be distinguished from linen. He also describes "how the Scythians exposed themselves as in a bath" to the vapour of the seeds thrown on hot coals.

The hemp occurs in two principal forms, viz.: 1. *bhang*, consisting of the dried leaves and small stalks of a dark green colour, mixed with a few fruits. It has a peculiar odour but little taste. Mixed with flour or incorporated with sweetmeat it is called hashish. It is also smoked, or taken infused in cold water. 2. *Ganja* consists of the flowering shoots of the female plant, having a compound or glutinous appearance, and is brownish-green in colour.

Of the many curious experiences that have been written describing the effects of hashish, perhaps the most accurate is that given by Gautier, in which he relates his own experience of the drug.

"The Orientalists," he states, "have in consequence of the interdiction of wine sought that species of excitement which the Western nations derive from alcoholic drinks." He then proceeds to state how a few minutes after swallowing some of the preparation, a sudden overwhelming sensation took possession of him. It appeared to him that his body was dissolved, and that he had become transparent. He clearly saw in his stomach the hashish he had swallowed, under the form of an emerald, from which a thousand little sparks issued. His eyelashes were lengthened out indefinitely, and rolled like threads of gold around ivory balls, which turned with inconceivable rapidity. Around him were sparklings of precious stones of all colours, changes eternally produced, like the play of a kaleidoscope. He every now and then saw his friends who were round him, disfigured as half men, half plants, some having the wings of the ostrich, which they were constantly shaking. So strange were these that he burst into fits of laughter, and, to join in the apparent ridiculousness of the affair, he began by throwing the cushions in the air, catching and turning them with the rapidity of an Indian juggler. One gentleman spoke to him in Italian, which the hashish transposed into Spanish. After a few minutes he recovered his habitual calmness, without any bad effect, and only with feelings of astonishment at what had passed. Half an hour had scarcely elapsed before he again fell under the influence of the drug. On this occasion the vision was more complicated and extraordinary. In the air there were millions of butterflies, confusedly luminous, shaking their wings like fans. Gigantic flowers, with chalices of crystal; large peonies upon beds of gold and silver, rose and surrounded him with the crackling sound that accompanies the explosion in the air of fireworks. His hearing acquired new power; it was enormously developed. He heard the noise of colours. Green, red, blue, yellow sounds reached him in waves—a glass thrown down, the creaking of a sofa, a word pronounced low, vibrated and rolled within him like peals of thunder. His own voice sounded so loud that he feared to speak, lest he should knock down the walls or explode like a rocket. More than five hundred clocks struck the hour with fleeting silvery voice, and every object touched gave a note like the harmonica or the Æolian harp. He swam in an ocean of sound, where floated like aisles of light some of the airs of "Lucia di Lammermoor" and the "Barber of Seville." Never did similar bliss overwhelm him with its waves; he was lost in a wilderness of sweets; he was not himself; he was relieved from consciousness, that feeling which always pervades the mind; and for the first time he comprehended what might be the state of elementary beings, of angels, of souls separated from the body. All his system seemed infected with the fantastic colouring in which he wasplunged. Sounds, perfume, light, reached him only by minute rays, in the midst of which he heard mystic currents whistling along. According to his calculation, this state lasted about three hundred years, for the sensations were so numerous and so hurried one upon the other, that a real appreciation of time was impossible. The paroxysm over, he was aware that it had only lasted *a quarter of an hour*.

Another interesting account of the strange hallucinations produced by the drug is related by Dr. Moreau, who with two friends experimented with hashish. "At first," he states, "I thought my companions were less influenced by the drug than myself. Then, as the effect increased, I fancied that the person who had brought me the dose had given me some of more active quality. This, I thought to myself, was an imprudence, and the involuntary idea presented itself that I might be poisoned. The idea became fixed; I called out loudly to Dr. Roche, 'You are an assassin; you have poisoned me!' This was received with shouts of laughter, and my lamentations excited mirth. I struggled for some time against the thought, but the greater the effort the more completely did it overcome me, till at last it took full possession of my mind. The extravagant conviction now came uppermost that I was dead, and upon the point of being buried; my soul had left my body. In a few minutes I had gone through all the stages of delirium."

These fixed ideas and erroneous convictions are apt to be produced, but they only last a few seconds, unless there is any actual physical disorder. "The Orientalist, when he indulges in hashish retires into the depth of his harem; no one is then admitted who cannot contribute to his enjoyment. He surrounds himself with his dancing girls, who perform their graceful evolutions before him to the sound of music; gradually a new condition of the brain allows a series of illusions, arising from the external senses, to present themselves. The mind becomes overpowered by the brilliancy of gorgeous visions; discrimination, comparison, reason, yield up their throne to dreams and phantoms which exhilarate and delight.

"The mind tries to understand what is the cause of the new delight, but it is in vain. It seems to know there is no reality."

Hardly two people experience the same effects from hashish. Upon some it has little action, while upon others, especially women, it exerts extraordinary power. While one person says he imagined his body endowed with such elasticity, that he fancied he could enter into a bottle and remain there at his ease, another fancied he had become the piston of a steam engine; under the influence of the drug the ear lends itself more to the illusion than any other sense. Its first effect is one of intense exhilaration, almost amounting to delirium; power of thought is soon lost, and the victim laughs, cries and sings or dances, all the time imagining he is acting rationally. The second stage is one of dreamy enjoyment followed by a dead stupor.

Of the ordinary physical effects of hashish, the first is a feeling of slight compression of the temporal bones and upper parts of the head. The respiration is gentle, the pulse is increased, and a gentle heat is felt all over the surface of the body. There is a sense of weight about the fore part of the arms, and an occasional slight involuntary motion, as if to seek relief from it. There is a feeling of discomfort about the extremities, creating a feeling of uneasiness, and if the dose has been too large the usual symptoms of poisoning by Indian hemp show themselves. Flushes of heat seem to ascend, to the head, even to the brain, which create considerable alarm. Singing in the ears is complained of; then comes on a state of anxiety, almost of anguish, with a sense of constriction about the chest. The individual fancies he hears the beating of his heart with unaccustomed loudness; but throughout the whole period it is the nervous system that is affected, and in this way the drug differs materially from opium whose action on the muscular and digestive systems is most marked.

It is somewhat remarkable that Indian hemp fails to produce the same intoxicating effects in this country that it does in warmer climates, and whether this is due to the loss of some volatile principle or difference in temperature it is not yet determined. But would-be experimentalists in the effects of hashish would do well to remember that it may not be indulged in with impunity, and most authorities agree that the brain becomes eventually disordered with frequent indulgence in the drug even in India. It further becomes weakened and incapable of separating the true from the false; frequent intoxication leads to a condition of delirium, and usually of a dangerous nature; the moral nature becomes numbed, and the victim at last becomes unfit to pursue his ordinary avocation. It is stated by those who have had considerable experience in its use, that even during the dream of joy there is a consciousness that all is illusion; there is at no period a belief that anything that dances before the senses or plays upon the imagination is real, and that when the mind recovers its equilibrium it knows that all is but a phantasm.

CHAPTER XVIII

TOBACCO LORE

F<small>EW</small>, perchance, of the millions who gather comfort from the "herb of fragrance" are aware that it is to Don Hernandez de Toledo we are indebted for the introduction of tobacco into Western Europe, which he first brought to Spain and Portugal in 1559. Jean Nicot was at this time Ambassador at the Court of Lisbon from Frances II, and it was he who transmitted or carried, either the seed or the plant to Catherine de Medicis, and who gave it the name *Nicotiana*. Like other great personages of the time, Catherine encouraged the homage of travellers and artists. It was considered to be one of the wonders of the New World, and reported to possess most extraordinary medicinal properties and virtues. Thirty years later the Cardinal Santa Croce, returning from his nunciature in Spain and Portugal to Italy, took with him some tobacco leaves, and we may form some idea of the enthusiasm with which its production was hailed, from a perusal of the poetry which the subject inspired, such as the following:

Herb of immortal fame!

Which hither first with Santa Croce came,

When he, his time of nunciature expired,

Back from the Court of Portugal retired;

Even as his predecessor, great and good,

Brought home the cross.

The poet compares the exploit of the cardinal with that of his progenitor, who brought home the wood of the true cross.

The first exact description of the plant is that given by Gonzalo Fernandez de Oviedo-y-Valdés, Governor of St. Domingo, in his *Historia General de las Indias*, printed at Seville in 1535. In this work, the leaf is said to be smoked through a branched tube of the shape of the letter Y, which the natives called *tobaco*.

After the introduction of tobacco into England by Sir Walter Raleigh on his return from America, the custom of smoking the leaf became very general, and it truly seems to have supplied a common want. It was mostly sold by the apothecaries in their dark little shops, and here the gallants would congregate to smoke their pipes and gossip, while the real Timidado, nicotine cane and pudding, was cut off with a silver knife on a maple block and retailed to the customers. The pipes used in the time of Queen Elizabeth were chiefly made of silver. The commoner kinds consisted of a walnut shell, in which a straw was inserted, and the tobacco was sold in the shops for its weight in silver.

The celebrated *Counterblaste to Tobacco*, by King James I, describes smoking as "a custom loathsome to the eye, hatefull to the nose, harmfull to the brain, dangerous to the lungs; and in the black, stinking fume thereof, nearest resembling the horrible Stygian smoake of the pit that is bottomlesse." In 1604 this monarch endeavoured, by means of heavy imposts, to abolish its use in this country, and in 1619 he commanded that no planter in Virginia should cultivate more than one hundred pounds.

It is said, some spent as much as £500 a year in the purchase of tobacco in those days. In 1624 Pope Urban VIII published a decree of excommunication against all who took snuff in the church. Ten years after this, smoking was forbidden in Russia under pain of having the nose cut off; and in 1653 the Council of the Canton of Appenzell cited smokers before them, whom they punished, ordering all innkeepers to inform against such as were found smoking in their houses. The police regulations made in Berne in 1661 were divided according to the Ten Commandments, in which the prohibition of smoking stands after the command against adultery. This prohibition was renewed in 1675, and the tribunal instituted to put it into execution—viz., Chambreau Tabac—continued to the middle of the eighteenth century. Pope Innocent XII, in 1690, excommunicated all those who were found taking snuff or tobacco in the Church of St. Peter at Rome; and even so late as 1719 the Senate of Strasburg prohibited the cultivation of tobacco, from an apprehension that it would diminish the growth cf corn. Amurath IV published an edict which made smoking tobacco a capital offence; but, notwithstanding all opposition, its fascinating power has held its own.

It is believed that the tobacco plant *Nicotiana Tabacum* is a native of tropical America, and it was found by the Spaniards when they landed in Cuba in 1492. There seems little doubt that the practice of smoking the leaf has been common among the natives of South America from time immemorial. It is now cultivated all over the world, but nowhere more abundantly or with better results than in the United States. Virginia is perhaps most celebrated for its culture. The young shoots produced from seeds thickly sown in beds, are transplanted into the fields during the month of May, and set in rows, with an interval of three or four feet between the plants. Through the whole period of its growth, the crop requires constant attention till the harvest time, in the month of August. The ripe plants having been cut off above their roots, are dried under cover, and then stripped of their leaves, which are tied in bundles and packed in hogsheads. While hung up in the drying-houses, they undergo a curing process, consisting of exposure to a considerable degree of heat, through which they become moist, after which they are dried for packing. In Persia and Turkey a form of tobacco is sold under the name of Tumbeki for use in the water-pipes or narghileh, which is said to be the product of the *Nicotiana Persica.*

The active principle *Nicotine* was first isolated in 1828, by Posselt and Reimann, and is an almost colourless, oily liquid of a highly poisonous nature. It soon becomes brown on exposure to air or light. The amount present in tobacco leaves varies considerably, but it is usually about six per cent. It has not been met with in tobacco smoke, according to Vohl, but the tobacco oils contain minute proportion of nicotine. One drop of pure nicotine is sufficient to kill a dog, while a very little more will destroy life in a human being. It is said to possess the property of resisting decomposition amid the decaying tissues of the body, and was detected by Orfila two or three months after death. Vohl and Eulenberg have made an interesting investigation of tobacco smoke. The smoke analysed was from a tobacco containing four per cent. of nicotine, but none of the alkaloid was found in the smoke. In the smoke of cigars certain gases were given off, and an oily body collected, which, on distillation, yielded aromatic acids. Distilled at a temperature above boiling water, tobacco gives an empyreumatic oil of a poisonous nature. It exactly resembles that which collects in the stems of tobacco pipes, and contains a small percentage of nicotine. The actual amount of nicotine absorbed into the blood while smoking a pipe is very minute, at least fifty per cent. of the entire alkaloid being destroyed by decomposition, and escaping from the bowl of the pipe. The habitual inhalation of tobacco smoke is undoubtedly harmful, but unless the smoke be intentionally inhaled, very little makes its way into the lungs. A great deal of misconception exists in the mind of the average individual as to the power of the alkaloid of tobacco. The amount of nicotine actually absorbed from a fair-sized pipe is about one- fortieth of a grain, in a cigar rather less. Death has resulted after smoking eighteen pipes, and from twenty cigars smoked continuously.

Tobacco is a powerful sedative poison; used in large quantities it causes vertigo, stupor, faintness, and general depression of the nervous system. It will sometimes cause excessive nausea and retching, with feebleness of pulse, coolness of the skin, and occasionally convulsions. But there seems very little known as to how these symptoms are produced. Employed to excess, it enfeebles digestion, produces emaciation and general debility, and is often the beginning of serious nervous disorders. Be this as it may, the moderate smoking of tobacco has, in most cases, even beneficial results, and there appears little doubt that it acts as a solace and comfort to the poor as well as the rich. It soothes the restless, calms mental and corporeal inquietude, and produces a condition of repose without a corresponding reaction or after-effect. In adults, especially those liable to mental worry, and all brain workers, its action is often a boon, the only danger being in overstepping the boundary of moderation to excess. It is not suitable to every constitution, and those who can trace to it evil effects should not continue its use.

CHAPTER XIX

POISON HABITS

T<small>HERE</small> is a very peculiar property attached to poisons, especially those possessing anodyne properties—that is, they are capable of forming the most enslaving habits known to mankind. Thousands of people to-day are enchained in the slavery of the poison habit in one form or another, and very few are ever successful in wresting them selves free when once it has been contracted. The habit is formed in the most insidious manner. Often, in the first instance, some narcotic drug is recommended to relieve pain or induce sleep. In a short time the original dose fails to produce the desired effect, it has to be increased, and afterwards still further increased, until the victim finds he cannot do without it, and a terrible craving for the drug is created. By-and-by the stupefying action affects the brain, the moral character suffers, and the unfortunate being is at last ready to do anything to obtain a supply of the drug that is now his master.

This is not an overdrawn picture, but one of which instances are constantly to be met with. The enslaving habit of alcohol, when once contracted, is too well known to need description. Opium comes next in the point of influence it exerts over its victims, and a very small percentage ever free themselves from the habit when it is once contracted. In most instances it is taken in the first place to relieve some severe pain, as in De Quincey's case. He says, in his *Confessions of an Opium Eater*, "It was not for the purpose of creating pleasure, but of mitigating pain in the severest degree, that I first began to use opium as an article of daily diet." Like others, he was compelled to increase the dose gradually, until at last he consumed the enormous quantity of 320 grains of the drug a day. He graphically describes the struggle he first had to reduce the daily dose, and found that to a certain point it could be reduced with ease, but after that point, further reduction caused intense suffering. However, a crisis arrived, and he writes, "I saw that I must die if I continued the opium. I determined, therefore, if that should be required, to die in throwing it off. I apprehend at this time I was taking from 50 or 60 grains to 150 grains a day. My first task was to reduce it to 40, to 30, and as fast as I could to 12 grains. I triumphed; but think not my sufferings were ended. Think of me, as one, even when four months had passed, still agitated, writhing, throbbing, palpitating, shattered; and much perhaps in the situation of him who has been racked." Other cases are commonly met with in this country, where opium eaters take on an average from 60 to 80 grains of the drug a day. The smallest quantity which has proved fatal in the adult is 4½ grains; in other cases enormous quantities have been taken with impunity; and Guy states recovery once took place after no less than eight ounces of solid opium had been swallowed.

Morphine, the chief alkaloid of opium, is also abused by many, and is swallowed as well as used by injection under the skin. Its action is very similar to that of opium. It has been recently given on good authority, that in Chicago—that city of hurrying men and restless women—over thirty-five thousand persons habitually take subcutaneous injections of morphine to save themselves from the pains and terrors of neuralgia, insomnia, and nervousness, etc. To a delicate woman one grain of this drug has proved fatal, yet, under the influence of habit, a young lady has been known to take from 15 to 20 grains daily. A man in a good position, and head of a large commercial house, contracted the habit of taking morphine from a prescription he had had given to him containing 4 grains of the drug. As the habit grew, he would have the medicine prepared by four different chemists daily, and swallow the contents of each bottle for a dose, until he took on an average over 24 grains a day. This being put a stop to by his friends, he commenced to take chloroform, which he would purchase in small quantities until he had collected a bottleful, and then he would drink it, usually mixed with whisky. He eventually had to be placed under restraint.

Chloroform is not often taken habitually, but several instances have been met with where as much as two ounces have been swallowed by a man. The effects, when taken by the mouth, are similar to those which follow its inhalation. Chlorodyne, which generally contains both morphine and prussic acid in its composition, is also much abused, especially by women. Some women have been known to consume two ounces a week of this preparation. Cocaine, an active principle of the *Erythroxylum coca*, is capable of exciting a powerful craving, which apparently holds its victims in a grip of iron until they are willing to spend any amount of money in obtaining the drug. Arsenic eating is a habit fortunately rare in this country, although cases have been met with in which women have gradually become addicted to taking large quantities for improving their complexions. The peasants in some parts of Styria and Hungary have long been known to eat arsenic, taking, it is said, from two to five grains daily; the men doing so in order that they may gain strength and be able to endure fatigue, and the women that they may improve their complexions. Dr. Maclagan, of Edinburgh, states he saw a Styrian eat a piece of arsenious acid weighing over four grains.

Sleeplessness is a frequent cause of the formation of a poison habit, and for this purpose chloral hydrate, perhaps, is capable of producing more serious results than any other drug of its class. The fact that it accumulates in the system, and that the dose needs constantly to be increased, always renders its use dangerous in unskilled hands. Many gifted men have fallen victims to the habit, among others Dante Rossetti, who seldom was without a bottle of the narcotic near him. Latterly, sulphonal, a drug derived from coal tar, possessing hypnotic properties, has been largely taken; and antipyrine, now a popular remedy for headache, is capable of forming a pernicious and dangerous habit. The practice of self-dosing with drugs of this description cannot be too strongly deprecated.

Some people form a curious habit of taking one drug till at last they become imbued with the idea that that only and nothing else, will have any effect on them. The only remedy Carlyle would ever take, according to the late Sir Richard Quain who was his medical adviser, was Grey powder. "Grey powder was his favourite remedy when he had that wretched dyspepsia from which he suffered, and which was fully accounted for by the fact that he was particularly fond of very nasty gingerbread. Many times I have seen him, sitting in the chimney corner, smoking a clay pipe and eating this gingerbread." Oliver Goldsmith also laboured under the confirmed belief that the only medicine that would have any effect on him was "James' Powder." He doctored himself with this favourite nostrum whenever he felt unwell, and believed it to be a cure for all ills.

According to a West End physician quite a new and most reprehensible vice has recently become fashionable—viz., a craze that has arisen among women for smoking green tea, in the form of cigarettes. Though adopted by some fair ladies merely as a pastime, not a few of its votaries are women of high education and mental attainments. "Among my patients," he states, "suffering from extreme nervousness and insomnia, is a young lady, highly distinguished, at Girton. Another is a lady novelist, whose books are widely read, and who habitually smoked twenty or thirty of these cigarettes nightly when writing, for their stimulating effect." Though tea does not contain a trace of any poisonous principle, it can, when thus misused, exert a most harmful influence. Doubtless, the high pressure at which most of the dwellers in our great cities now live, and the worry of too much brain work on one hand, or the lack of occupation on the other, is one of the chief causes of taking up habits of this kind.

One of the best remedies, and one which it is to be hoped will eventually come to pass is, that the Legislature should render poisons less easy of purchase, by restricting the sale of every drug or compound in the nature of a poison to the properly qualified chemist, who, by his training and special knowledge, is alone competent to sell these substances. Incalculable harm is done by habits such as we have alluded to, and it is better often to endure pain and torment, than to fly constantly to what in the end will only inflict worse punishment.

———————————————

CHAPTER XX

F$_{ROM}$ a very early period poisoning mysteries have been woven into romance and story, and in later times have been a favourite theme for both novelist and dramatist. But unfortunately, the scientific knowledge of writers of fiction, as a rule, is of a very limited description, and the effects attributed by them to certain drugs are usually as fabulous as the romances of the olden times. They tell us of mysterious poisons of untold power, an infinitesimal quantity of which will cause instantaneous death without leaving a trace behind. They describe anæsthetics so powerful, that a whiff from a bottle is sufficient to produce immediate insensibility for any period desired. In fact, the novelist has a pharmacopœia of his own. After all, why should we question or cavil, and wish to analyse it in the prosaic test tube of modern science; for take away the marvels and mysteries and you kill the romance. The novel performs its mission if it succeeds in interesting and amusing us, and the story-teller has accomplished the object of his art when he is successful in weaving the possible with the impossible, so that we can scarce perceive it.

That master of fiction, Dumas, gives us an instance of this, in his wonderfully fascinating adventures of the Count Monte Christo. Nothing seems impossible to this extraordinary individual, and incident after incident of the most romantic and exciting nature crowd one upon another throughout the story; yet so beautifully blended by the wonderful imagination of the author, that it enthrals us to the end. The Count, who is supposed to have studied the art of medicine in the East, has always a remedy at hand for every emergency, from hashish, in which he is a profound believer, to his mysterious stimulating elixir, described as "of the colour of blood, preserved in a phial of Bohemian glass." A single drop of this marvellous fluid, if allowed to fall on the lips, will, almost before it reaches them, restore the marble and inanimate form to life. His pill boxes were composed of emeralds and precious stones of huge size, and their contents consisted of drugs, whose effects were beyond conception. His knowledge of chemistry and toxicology is equally astonishing, as instanced in the conversation he holds with Madame de Villefort, who, for nefarious purposes, desires to improve her knowledge of poisons. Monte Christo discourses on the poisonous properties of brucine, a drug rarely used in England, but largely used in France. "Suppose," says the Count, "you were to take a millegramme of this poison the first day, two millegrammes the second day, and so on. Well, at the end of ten days you would have taken a centigramme: at the end of twenty days, increasing another millegramme, you would have taken three hundred centigrammes; that is to say, a dose you would support without inconvenience, and which would be very dangerous for any other person who had not taken the same precautions as yourself. Well, then, at the end of a month, when drinking water from the same carafe, you would kill the person who had drunk this water, without your perceiving otherwise than from slight inconvenience that there was any poisonous substance mingled with the water." The Count thus explains the doctrine of immunity from a poison, by accustoming the system to its effect in small doses for a length of time, a process which is actually possible with some drugs, but not with all. His satirical description of the bungling of the common poisoner, as compared to the fine subtlety and cunning he advocates, is also worth quoting: "Amongst us a simpleton, possessed by the demon of hate or cupidity, who has an enemy to destroy, or some near relation to dispose of, goes straight to the grocer's or druggist's, gives a false name, which leads more easily to his detection than his real one, and purchases, under a pretext that the rats prevent him from sleeping, five or six pennyworth of arsenic. If he is really a cunning fellow he goes to five or six different druggists or grocers, and thereby becomes only five or six times more easily traced; then, when he has acquired his specific, he administers duly to his enemy or near kinsman a dose of arsenic which would make a mammoth or mastodon burst, and which, without rhyme or reason, makes his victim utter groans which alarm the whole neighbourhood. Then arrive a crowd of policemen and constables. They fetch a doctor, who opens the dead body, and collects from the entrails and stomach a quantity of arsenic in a spoon. Next day a hundred newspapers relate the fact, with the names of the victim and the murderer. The same evening the grocer or grocers, druggist or druggists, come and say, 'It was I who sold the arsenic to the gentleman accused'; and rather than not recognize the guilty purchaser, they will recognize twenty. Then the foolish criminal is taken, imprisoned, interrogated, confronted, confounded, condemned, and cut off by hemp or steel; or, if she be a woman of any consideration, they lock her up for life. This is the way in which you northerners understand chemistry." And so he endeavours to incite a woman, who is already anxiously contemplating a series of terrible crimes.

The recital of the ingenious experiments of the Abbé Adelmonte is a piece of clever construction, as the quotation will show. "The Abbé," said Monte Christo, "had a remarkably fine garden full of vegetables, flowers, and fruit. From amongst these vegetables he selected the most simple—a cabbage, for instance. For three days he watered this cabbage with a distillation of arsenic; on the third, the cabbage began to droop and turn yellow. At that moment he cut it. In the eyes of everybody it seemed fit for table, and preserved its wholesome appearance. It was only poisoned to the Abbé Adelmonte. He then took the cabbage to the room where he had rabbits, for the Abbé Adelmonte had a collection of rabbits, cats, and guinea-pigs, equally fine as his collection of vegetables, flowers, and fruit. Well, the Abbé Adelmonte took a rabbit and made it eat a leaf of the cabbage. The rabbit died. What magistrate would find or even venture to insinuate anything against this? What *procureur du roi* has ever ventured to draw up an accusation against M. Magendie or M. Flourens, in consequence of the rabbits, cats, and guinea-pigs they have killed? Not one. So, then, the rabbit dies, and justice takes no notice. This rabbit dead, the Abbé Adelmonte has its entrails taken out by his cook and thrown on the dunghill; on this dunghill was a hen, who, pecking these intestines, was, in her turn, taken ill, and dies next day. At the moment when she was struggling in the convulsions of death, a vulture was flying by (there are a good many vultures in Adelmonte's country); this bird darts on the dead bird and carries it away to a rock, where it dines off its prey. Three days afterwards this poor vulture, who has been very much indisposed since that dinner, feels very giddy, suddenly, whilst flying aloft in the clouds, and falls heavily into a fish- pond. The pike, eels, and carp eat greedily always, as everybody knows— well, they feast on the vulture. Well, suppose the next day, one of these eels, or pike, or carp is served at your table, poisoned, as they are to the third generation. Well, then, your guest will be poisoned in the fifth generation, and die at the end of eight or ten days, of pains in the intestines, sickness, or abscess of the pylorus. The doctors open the body, and say, with an air of profound learning, 'The subject has died of a tumour on the liver, or typhoid fever.'"

After attempting to kill half the household with brucine, Madame de Villefort changes her particular poison for a simple narcotic, recognized by Monte Christo (who in this instance frustrates the murderer) as being dissolved in alcohol. The name of the latter poison is not told us by the novelist, but on the doctor's examination of the suspected liquid we read, "He took from its silver case a small bottle of nitric acid, dropped a little of it into the liquor, which immediately changed to a blood-red colour."

Perhaps the most curious method of poisoning ever used in fiction is that introduced by the late Mr. James Payn in his novel, "Halves." The poisoner uses finely chopped horse-hair as a medium for getting rid of her niece. In this way she brings on a disease which puzzles the doctor, until one day he comes across the would-be murderess pulling the horse-hair out of the drawing-room sofa, which causes him to suspect her at once. This ingenious lady introduced the chopped horse-hair into the pepper-pot used by her victim. The inimitable Count Fosco, whom Wilkie Collins introduces into "The Woman in White," was supposed to possess a remarkable knowledge of chemistry, although he says, "Only twice did I call science to my aid," in working out his plot to abduct Lady Glyde. His media were simple: "A medicated glass of water and a medicated bottle of smelling-salts relieved her of all further embarrassment and alarm." This genial villain waxes eloquent on the science of chemistry in his confession. "Chemistry!" he exclaims, "has always had irresistible attractions for me from the enormous, the illimitable power which the knowledge of it confers. Chemists—I assert it emphatically—might sway, if they pleased, the destinies of humanity. Mind, they say, rules the world. But what rules the mind? The body (follow me closely here) lies at the mercy of the most omnipotent of all potentates—the chemist. Give me—Fosco—chemistry; and when Shakespeare has conceived Hamlet, and sits down to execute the conception—with a few grains of powder dropped into his daily food, I will reduce his mind, by the action of his body, till his pen pours out the most abject drivel that has ever degraded paper. Under similar circumstances revive me the illustrious Newton. I guarantee that when he sees the apple fall he shall *eat it*, instead of discovering the principle of gravitation. Nero's dinner shall transform Nero into the mildest of men before he has done digesting it, and the morning draught of Alexander the Great shall make Alexander run for his life at the first sight of the enemy the same afternoon. On my sacred word of honour it is lucky for Society that modern chemists are, by incomprehensible good fortune, the most harmless of mankind. The mass are worthy fathers of families, who keep shops. The few are philosophers besotted with admiration for the sound of their own lecturing voices, visionaries who waste their lives on fantastic impossibilities, or quacks whose ambition soars no higher than our corns."

In "Armadale," the same novelist introduces us to a poisoner of the deepest dye in the person of Miss Gwilt. This fair damsel, whose auburn locks seemed to have possessed an irresistible attraction for the opposite sex, was addicted to taking laudanum to soothe her troubled nerves, and first tried to mix a dose with some lemonade she had prepared for her husband's namesake and friend, whom she wished out of the way. This attempt failing, and a second one, to scuttle a yacht in which he was sailing, proving futile also, he was finally lured to a sanatorium in London, where she had arranged for him to be placed to sleep in a room into which a poisonous gas (presumably carbonic acid) was to be passed. At the last moment she discovers her husband has taken the place of her victim, and in a revulsion of feeling she rescues him, and ends her own life instead in the poisoned chamber. According to the story, the medical investigation which followed this tragedy ended in discovering that she had died of apoplexy; a fact which had it occurred in real life would not have redounded to the credit of the medical men who conducted it.

The heroine of Mr. Benson's novel, "The Rubicon," poisons herself with prussic acid of <u>unheard of</u> strength, which she discovers *among some photographic chemicals.*

On the stage, "poisoning" has gone somewhat out of fashion with modern dramatists, although it was a common thing in years gone by for the villain of the play to swallow a cup of cold poison in the last act, and after several dying speeches to fall suddenly flat on his back and die to slow music. The death of Cleopatra, described by Shakespeare as resulting from the bite of a venomous snake, is like no clinical description of the final effects of death from the bite of any known snake. Beverley, in "The Gamester," takes a dose of strong poison in the fifth act, and afterwards makes several fairly long speeches before he apparently feels the effects, and finally succumbs. The description of the death of Juliet, which Shakespeare, in all probability, conceived from reading the effects that followed the drinking of morion or mandragora wine, is an accurate description of death from that drug. The use of this anodyne preparation to deaden pain dates from ancient times, and it is stated it was a common practice for women to administer it to those about to suffer the penalty of the law by being crucified. We have another instance of the fabulous effects ascribed to poisons by the early playwrights, in Massinger's play, "The Duke of Milan." Francisco dusts over a plant some poisonous powder and hands it to Eugenia. Ludovico approaches, and kisses the lady's hand but twice, and then dies from the effects of the poison.

Miss Helen Mathers, in one of her recent works, viz., "The Sin of Hagar," a story warranted to thrill the soul of "Sweet Seventeen," makes some extraordinary discoveries which will be new to chemists. For instance, she tells us of strychnine that actually *discolours* a glass of whisky and water. One of the characters, a frisky old dowager, professes to be an *amateur* chemist, and this lady, we are gravely informed by the novelist, "detects the presence of the strychnine in the glass of whisky and water *at a glance.*"

But Miss Mathers has still another poison, whose properties will doubtless be a revelation to scientists, and it is with this marvellous body the "double-dyed villainess" of the story puts an end to her woes. For convenience she carries it about with her concealed in a ring, and when at last she decides on committing suicide, we are told "she simply placed the ring to her lips, a strange odour spread through the room, and she instantly lay dead."

Sufficient eccentricities of this kind in fiction might be enumerated to fill a volume, but we must forbear. It is perhaps hardly necessary to state that the lady novelist is the greatest sinner in this respect, and stranger poisons are evolved from her fertile brain than were ever known to man.

CHAPTER XXI

T̲OWARDS̲ the close of the year 1891 and the early part of 1892, public interest was excited by the mysterious deaths of several young women of the "unfortunate" class residing in the neighbourhood of Lambeth. The first case was that of a girl named Matilda Clover, who lived in Lambeth Road. On the night of October 20, 1891, she spent the evening at a music-hall in company with a man, who returned with her to her lodgings about nine o'clock. Shortly afterwards she was seen to go out alone, and she purchased some bottled beer, which she carried to her rooms. After a little time the man left the house.

At three o'clock in the morning the inmates of the house were aroused by the screams of a woman, and on the landlady entering Matilda Clover's room, she found the unfortunate girl lying across the bed in the greatest agony. Medical aid was sent for, and the assistant of a neighbouring doctor saw the girl, and judged she was suffering from the effects of drink. He prescribed a sedative mixture, but the girl got worse, and, after a further convulsion, died on the following morning. The medical man whose assistant had seen her the previous night, gave a certificate that death was due to delirium tremens and syncope, and Matilda Clover was buried at Tooting.

A few weeks afterwards a woman called Ellen Donworth, who resided in Duke Street, Westminster Bridge Road, is stated to have received a letter, in consequence of which she went out between six and seven in the evening. About eight o'clock she was found in Waterloo Road in great agony, and died while she was being conveyed to St. Thomas's Hospital. Before her death she made a statement, that a man with a dark beard and wearing a high hat had given her "two drops of white stuff" to drink. In this case a post-mortem examination was made and on analysis both strychnine and morphine were found in the stomach, proving that the woman had been poisoned.

These cases had almost been forgotten, when, some six months afterwards, attention was again aroused by the mysterious deaths of two girls named Alice Marsh and Emma Shrivell, who lodged in Stamford Street. On the evening of April 11, 1892, a man, who one of the girls in her dying testimony called "Fred," and who she described as a doctor, called to see them, and together they partook of tea. The man stayed till 2 a.m., and during the evening gave them both "three long pills."

Half an hour after the man left the house, both girls were found in a dying condition. While they were being removed to the hospital Alice Marsh died in the cab, and Emma Shrivell lived for only six hours afterwards. The result of an analysis of the stomach and organs revealed the fact that death in each case had been caused by strychnine.

There was absolutely no evidence beyond the vague description of the man for the police to work upon, and this case, like the others, with which at first it was not connected, seemed likely to remain among the unsolved mysteries; when by the following curious chain of circumstances, the perpetrator of these cold-blooded crimes was at last brought to justice.

Some time after the deaths of the two girls Marsh and Shrivell, a Dr. Harper, of Barnstaple, received a letter, in which the writer stated, that he had indisputable evidence that the doctor's son, who had recently qualified as a medical practitioner in London, had poisoned two girls—Marsh and Shrivell —and that he, the writer, required £1,500 to suppress it. Dr. Harper placed this letter in the hands of the police, with the result. that on June 3, 1892, a man named Thomas Neill, or Neill Cream, was arrested on the charge of sending a threatening letter. He was brought up at Bow Street on this charge for several days, when it transpired that in the preceding November a well- known London physician had also received a letter, in which the writer declared that he had evidence to show that the physician had poisoned a Miss Clover with strychnine, which evidence he could purchase for £2,500, and so save himself from ruin.

Neill Cream was remanded, and in the meanwhile the body of Matilda Clover was exhumed, and the contents of the stomach sent to Dr. Stevenson, one of the Government analysts, for examination. He discovered the presence of strychnine, and came to the conclusion that some one had administered a fatal dose to her.

An inquest was then held on the body of Matilda Clover, with the result that James Neill, or Neill Cream, was committed on the charge of wilful murder.

This man's lodgings were searched after his arrest, and a curious piece of paper was discovered, on which, written in pencil in his handwriting, were the initials "M. C.," and opposite to them two dates, and then a third date, viz. October 20, which was the date of Matilda Clover's death. On the same paper, in connection with the initials "E. S.," was also found two dates, one being April 11, which was the date of Emma Shrivell's death. There was also found in his possession a paper bearing the address of Marsh and Shrivell, and it was afterwards proved that he had said on more than one occasion that he knew them well.

In his room a quantity of small pills were discovered, each containing from one-sixteenth to one-twenty-second of a grain of strychnine, also fifty-four other bottles of pills, seven of which contained strychnine, and a bottle containing one hundred and sixty-eight pills, each containing one-twenty-second of a grain of strychnine. These, it is supposed, he obtained as an agent for the Harvey Drug Co. of America. It was found he had purchased a quantity of empty gelatine capsules from a chemist in Parliament Street, which there is little doubt he had used to administer a number of the small pills in a poisonous dose.

Thomas Neill, or Neill Cream, was tried for the wilful murder of Matilda Clover at the Central Criminal Court, before Mr. Justice Hawkins, on October 18, 1892, the trial lasting five days.

It transpired that Cream, who had received some medical education and styled himself a "doctor," came to this country from America on October 1, 1891, and on arriving in London first stayed at Anderton's Hotel, in Fleet Street. Shortly afterwards he took apartments in Lambeth, and became engaged to a lady living at Berkhampstead.

He was identified as having been seen in the company of Matilda Clover, and also by a policeman, as the man who left the house in Stamford Street on the night that Marsh and Shrivell were murdered.

Dr. Stevenson, who made the analysis of the body of Matilda Clover on May 6, 1892, stated in his evidence that he found strychnine in the stomach, liver, and brain, and that quantitatively he obtained one-sixteenth of a grain of strychnine from two pounds of animal matter. He also examined the organs from the bodies of Alice Marsh and Emma Shrivell. He found 6·39 grains of strychnine in the stomach and its contents of Alice Marsh, and 1·6 grain of strychnine in the stomach and its contents, also 1·46 grain in the vomit, and ·2 grain in a small portion of the liver of Emma Shrivell.

The jury, after deliberating for ten minutes, returned a verdict of guilty, and Thomas Neill, or Neill Cream, as he was otherwise known, was sentenced to death. He was executed on November 15, 1892.

CHAPTER XXII

TOWARDS the close of the year 1897, a Mrs. Holmes, a widow, was living with her three children at Stoneley, near Kimbolton. She had a cousin named Walter Horsford, a well-to-do young farmer who occupied a farm at Spaldwick about twelve miles away, and who frequently came to Stoneley to visit her.

A romantic attachment eventually sprang up between them, which resulted in a too intimate acquaintance.

After a while Horsford's affection began to wane, and in the end he married another lady.

Shortly afterwards Mrs. Holmes left Stoneley and took up her residence at St. Neots.

About December of the same year she wrote a letter to Horsford, informing him of her condition, a piece of news which appears to have greatly upset him, as he was in fear the information might reach his wife.

On December 28 he called at a chemist's shop in Thrapstone, a neighbouring town, and asked for a shilling's worth of strychnine, some prussic acid, arsenic, and carbolic acid, which he stated he required for poisoning rats. The chemist, to whom he was a stranger, requested him to bring a witness, which he did, and the chemist's poison register was duly signed by Horsford and a man who introduced him. He took the poisons, which consisted of ninety grains of strychnine, one pound of arsenic, and some prussic acid and carbolic acid, away with him.

About a week afterwards Mrs. Holmes received a letter from Horsford. It was taken in by her daughter, who recognised his handwriting, and the envelope is also supposed to have contained two packets of strychnine.

On the evening of January 7, 1898, Mrs. Holmes retired to bed, apparently in her usual health, about half-past nine. The only other persons in the house were her daughter Annie, her son Percy, and her infant. The daughter noticed that her mother took a glass of water upstairs with her, which was an unusual circumstance. On going to her mother's bedroom shortly afterwards, she found her suffering great pain, and she saw the glass, now almost empty, standing on a chest of drawers.

Percy Holmes ran out and called in the assistance of some neighbours, and then went for a doctor. When medical aid arrived, the unfortunate woman was in convulsions and died shortly afterwards.

The day after her death the police searched the house, but failed to find any trace of poison, and an inquest was held on January 8, which Horsford was summoned to attend.

In his evidence before the coroner, he swore that he had neither written to nor seen the deceased woman. The medical evidence proved that death was caused by strychnine.

The inquest was adjourned for a week, and in the meanwhile Mrs. Holmes was buried. From information received by the police, a further search was made in the house, with the result that two packets were discovered under the feather bed in Mrs. Holmes' bedroom. One packet of buff-coloured paper was found to contain about thirty-three grains of strychnine in powder, on which was written the words, "One dose. Take as told," in Horsford's handwriting. On the second packet, the contents of which had been used, was written, "Take in a little water. It is quite harmless." This was also in Horsford's handwriting.

On January 10, Walter Horsford was arrested on the charge of perjury committed at the inquest, and it was resolved to have another examination made of the body of the deceased woman. On examination of further documents and letters discovered by the police, the charge of wilful murder was added to corrupt perjury against Horsford, and he was committed for trial.

The trial took place on June 2, 1898, at Huntingdon, before Mr. Justice Hawkins.

Dr. Stevenson stated in his evidence, he first made an analysis of a portion of the body of Mrs. Holmes on January 19, and extracted 1·31 grain of strychnine, but no other poison. Subsequently he examined the two packets discovered under the bed, and found one contained 33¾ grains of powdered strychnine, and the other, which presented the appearance of having had the powder shaken out, a few minute crystals of strychnine. In each case it was the pure alkaloid. The body was exhumed nineteen days after death, and he then made an analysis of all the chief organs, and obtained therefrom a total quantity of 3·69 grains of strychnine. Death usually occurred about half an hour after the commencement of the symptoms. He judged there could not have been less than ten grains of strychnine in the body at the time of death.

The jury found Walter Horsford guilty, and he was sentenced to death.

CHAPTER XXIII

THE GREAT AMERICAN POISON MYSTERY

O_{NE} of the most carefully planned murders by means of poison in modern times was investigated at the trial of Roland B. Molineux, who was charged with causing the death of Mrs. Catherine J. Adams in New York in 1899.

On November 10, 1898, a Mr. Henry C. Barnett, a produce booker, who was a member of the Knickerbocker Athletic Club, one of the most prominent social organizations in New York, received by post at the club a sample box of Kutnow's Powder. He was in the habit of taking this and similar preparations for simple ailments, and soon after receiving the box he took a dose of its contents. He became ill immediately afterwards, and was thought to be suffering from diphtheria. That he had a slight attack of this disease there is little doubt, as the fact was proved from a bacteriological examination made by his medical attendant. He left his bed earlier than the doctor advised, and died presumably of heart failure.

The contents of the box, however, were examined, which led to the discovery that the powder had been tampered with and mixed with cyanide of mercury; and although Mr. Barnett had died from natural causes, it seemed clear an attempt had been made to poison him by some one who knew he was in the habit of taking this powder. The investigation, however, does not appear to have been carried farther.

The next chapter in the story occurred in connection with a Mr. Harry Cornish, who occupied the position of physical director to the Knickerbocker Athletic Club.

A day or two before Christmas in the same year, a packet directed to him was delivered by post at his address. It contained a box, in which, on opening, he found at one end a silver article for holding matches or toothpicks; at the other end was a bottle labelled "Emerson's Bromo-seltzer," and between the two was packed some soft tissue paper.

Mr. Cornish was at first under the impression that some one had sent him the packet as a present. After removing the articles from the box, he threw it and the wrapper into his wastepaper basket, but on second thoughts he cut the address from the wrapper and kept it.

The bottle, labelled "Bromo-seltzer," which is a saline preparation well known in America, was sealed over the top and bore the usual revenue stamp. After tearing off the outside wrapper, Mr. Cornish placed the bottle and the silver holder on his desk.

On the following Sunday he remarked to his aunt, a Mrs. Catherine Adams, that he had received a present. Mrs. Adams and her daughter Mrs. Rogers joked him about it, saying he must have some admirer, and was afraid to bring his present home, as the sender's name was probably upon it. So on Tuesday night Mr. Cornish took the bottle and the silver holder home with him, and presented them to Mrs. Rogers, saying they were no use to him and she might have them.

The next morning Mrs. Adams complained of a headache, and her daughter suggested a dose of the Bromo-seltzer. Mr. Cornish was present, and mixed a teaspoonful of the preparation from the bottle with a glass of water, and gave it to his aunt. After drinking it she at once exclaimed, "My, how bitter that is!"

"Why, that's all right!" said Mr. Cornish, as he took a drink from the glass.

A few moments afterwards Mrs. Adams collapsed, and died within a short time. Mr. Cornish was seized with violent vomiting, which doubtless saved his life, and he recovered.

A post-mortem examination revealed the fact that Mrs. Adams had died from cyanide poisoning; and on the bottle of Bromo-seltzer being analysed the contents were found to have been mixed with cyanide of mercury.

For a long time the affair seemed a complete mystery, and the police investigations appeared likely to be fruitless. Then the particulars of the death of Mr. Barnett, who was Chairman of the House Committee of the Knickerbocker Club, were brought to light; and connecting them with the fact that Mr. Cornish was also a prominent member of the club, and had received the bottle of Bromo-seltzer by post in the same manner, it seemed highly probable that both the poisoned packets which contained cyanide of mercury, had been sent by the same hand.

Further examination proved that the bottle used was not a genuine Bromo-seltzer one, and that the label had been removed from a genuine bottle and carefully pasted on that sent to Mr. Cornish.

A firm of druggists in Cincinnati then came forward and stated, that as far back as May 31, 1898, they had received a written application signed "H. C. Barnett" for a sample box of pills, and another similar application on December 21, 1898, which was signed "H. Cornish."

Both these applications were found to be in the same handwriting, which was also strikingly similar to the address on the packet sent to Mr. Cornish, which he had fortunately kept. The address given by the applicant who called himself "H. C. Barnett," was 257, West Forty-second Street; New York, a place where private letter-boxes are rented for callers. The address given by the applicant signing himself "H. Cornish," was a similar place at 1,620, Broadway, in the same city. From these facts it seemed evident that an attempt had been made to poison both Barnett and Cornish by some one who knew them, and the poisoner had concealed his identity by employing the names of his intended victims.

The nature of the poison used, cyanide of mercury, was also a slight clue, as it is a substance which is not used in medicine and must in all probability have been specially prepared for the purpose, by some one with a good knowledge of chemistry.

At the coroner's inquest, which began on February 9, 1899, certain facts were elicited that tended to bring suspicion on Roland B. Molineux, who was also a member of the Knickerbocker Club and well acquainted with Barnett and Cornish. He was also known to have quarrelled with the latter. At the close of the inquest Molineux was arrested, and removed to the Tombs prison.

Owing to legal technicalities in the original indictment, which charged him with the murder of both Mr. Barnett and Mrs. Adams, he was twice liberated, and then for the third time arrested.

The trial of Molineux for the murder of Mrs. Adams was a memorable one, and lasted nearly three months. It began on November 14, 1899, at the Central Criminal Court, New York, and was not concluded till February 11, 1900.

The evidence was entirely circumstantial. Most of the experts in handwriting who were examined declared that the address on the packet sent to Mr. Cornish was in Molineux's writing, and that he had also written both applications to the druggists in Cincinnati. Further, Molineux was engaged as a chemist to a colour factory in which cyanide of mercury was used, which would enable him either to make or procure that special poison, from which only three other fatal cases had been recorded.

No witnesses were called for the defence, and the jury found Roland B. Molineux guilty of "murder in the first degree," which, according to American law, is murder with premeditation.

CHAPTER XXIV

T<small>HE</small> strange and curious methods employed by poisoners to accomplish their deadly purpose, form an interesting study to students of human nature. The poisoner generally sets to work on a preconceived and carefully thought-out plan, which he proceeds to carry out with all the cunning he possesses. The methods that can be employed to introduce a poisonous substance into the human body are necessarily limited; and although they are varied at times according to the ingenuity in which the deed is planned, we find the poisoner with all his craft shows but little originality, and the modes used in ancient times are repeated down through the centuries to the present day.

There seems little doubt that the earliest method employed by man was the poisoned weapon.

The use of the poisoned arrow-head by primitive man goes back to a period of remote antiquity. Among the cave remains of the palæolithic period, arrow- and spear-heads of bone have been found marked with depressions for containing poison, and this method of introducing poison seems to have been practised by most of the aboriginal races.

Arrow poisons were well known to the Greeks and their word "toxicon" signified a poisonous substance into which the arrow-"toxon" was dipped. Homer alludes to the use of poisoned arrows in the "Odyssey," and Ovid mentions the bile and blood of vipers as being employed to poison weapons. The Scythians and the tribes of the Caucasus were reputed to use Viper poison mixed with the serum of human blood that had decomposed. The Celts and the Gauls, according to Pliny, dipped their arrow-heads in hellebore juice; and down to the seventh century we find poisoned weapons were commonly used in Europe.

During the Middle Ages until the sixteenth century, the poisoned dagger or sword formed the favourite weapon of the assassin, and the preparation of the blade for this purpose was brought almost to a fine art in Spain. It is recorded that Lorenzo de Medici was stabbed with a poisoned dagger; and the Duke de Biscaglia, the second husband of the famous Lucrezia Borgia, nearly fell a victim to the assassin's knife on the steps of St. Peter's.

Of all other methods employed by poisoners, the administration of the lethal dose through the medium of food or drink seems ever to have been the favourite. The poisoned wine or cake recurs with a somewhat monotonous frequency in the history of the poisoner, from the earliest times down to the present day. Women especially seem to have been attracted by this mode of poisoning, a fact probably due to their control and direction of domestic matters, which rendered the introduction of a poisonous substance into food or drink an easy matter. Occasionally they have fallen victims to their own evil designs, as instanced in the case of Rosamond the wife of Helmichis, King of Lombardy, in the year 575. Wishing to rid herself of her husband, she gave him a cup of poisoned wine on coming from his bath. The king drank part of it, and suspecting its nature from the strange effect it produced, he insisted she should drink the remainder, with the result that both died shortly afterwards.

The Hindoos have an ingenious method of using powdered glass as a lethal agent, either by mixing it with sherbet or some kind of food. In such cases the substance acts by its irritant action on the stomach or intestines, while at the same time, if successful, no trace of poison can be discovered in the bodily organs.

A celebrated case in which this agent was used occurred in India in 1874, when the Gaekwar, or reigning prince of Baroda was tried for attempting to kill his political resident, Colonel Phayre, by administering powdered glass to him in sherbet.

The Gaekwar was tried before a court consisting of three Indian princes and three English judges, and was defended by the late Mr. Serjeant Ballantine. The princes returned a verdict of "Not proven," while the judges decided that he was guilty, with the result that the Gaekwar was deposed.

The sweetmeat was a favourite form employed to administer poison during the Middle Ages. Such confections were usually handed round to the guests after a meal in Italy. Princes and nobles frequently used this method of ridding themselves of an enemy; and if the plot failed in the first instance, they were always ready to try it again, for, as Cæsar Borgia is stated to have once exclaimed, "what has failed at dinner-time will succeed at supper-time." Catherine de Medici introduced this method into France, and her Florentine perfumers were said to be adepts in mixing arsenic with sweetmeats.

The poisoned flowers of mediæval romance, and poisoned gloves and boots, which figure so often in legend and story as lethal media, we must dismiss as mere fables of an age when the historian drew largely on his imagination.

The "poison ring," with its carefully concealed tiny spike, which was intended to penetrate the flesh of the victim, might perhaps have set up blood-poisoning, as would a similar wound if inflicted by a rusty nail.

The use of rings with secret receptacles to contain poisons we have already mentioned. Among the gems in the British Museum there is an onyx which has been hollowed out to form a receptacle for poison. The face of the stone is engraved with the head of a horned faun. To take the poison, it was only necessary to bite through the thin shell of the onyx and swallow the contents.

When the gold deposited by Camillus in the Capitol was taken away, it is recorded that the custodian responsible for it "broke the stone of his ring in his mouth," and died shortly afterwards.

The poisoners of the seventeenth century not content with introducing poison into wine and other drinks, sought to improve on this method, by preparing the goblet or cup in such a way, that it would impregnate any liquid that was placed in it.

There is record of one François Belot who made a speciality of this art, and, it is said, received a comfortable income therefrom; but he fitly ended his days by being broken on the wheel on June 10, 1679.

According to a contemporary writer, his secret method consisted in cramming a toad with arsenic, placing it in a silver goblet, and, after pricking its head, crushing it in the vessel. While this operation was being performed, certain charms were uttered.

"I know a secret," stated Belot, "such, that in doctoring a cup with a toad, and what I put into it, if fifty persons chanced to drink from it afterwards, even if it were washed and rinsed, they would all be done for, and the cup could only be purified by throwing it into a hot fire. After having thus poisoned the cup, I should not try it upon a human being, but upon a dog, and I should entrust the cup to nobody." And yet Belot's powers were believed in, and he enjoyed a substantial reputation in his day.

His boasting is on a par with that of the magician Blessis, who flourished about the same period. He declared to the world that he had discovered a method of manipulating mirrors in such a way that any one who looked in them received his death-blow!

The stories of the "poisoned shirt," which was a favourite medium with the poisoners of the seventeenth century, are not, however, without a substratum of fact.

The tail of the shirt was prepared by soaking it in a strong solution of arsenic or corrosive sublimate. The object was to produce a violent dermatitis, with ulceration about the perineum and neighbouring parts, which should compel the victim to keep his bed. Medical men would then be summoned in due course, and would probably judge the patient to be suffering from syphilis, and administer mercury in large quantities. The fatal dose could then be introduced at leisure.

The notorious La Bosse left on record her method of preparing the "poisoned shirt." The garment was first to be washed, and the tail then soaked in a strong solution of arsenic, so that it only looked "a little rusty," as if it had been ill-washed and was stiffer than usual. "The effect," she concludes, "it should produce on the wearer is a violent inflammation and intense pain, and that when one came to examine him, one would not detect anything."

The Duke of Savoy is said to have succumbed to the effects of a poisoned shirt of this kind.

Some time ago Dr. Nass, a French medical man, made some interesting experiments, with a view to testing the truth of these stories. He carefully shaved a portion of the left lumbar region of a guinea-pig, and gently rubbed the skin with a paste containing arsenic, in the proportion of one in ten. He repeated this operation several times during the day. Shortly afterwards the animal became prostrate, the eyes became dull, it assumed a cholera-like aspect, and in forty-eight hours died. The skin on which the paste had been applied remained unchanged and unbroken, and showed no sign of ulceration. On examining the internal organs after death, fatty degeneration of the viscera was found, as is usual after arsenical poisoning.

This experiment does not, of course, actually prove the effect of a shirt impregnated with arsenic being worn in direct contact with the skin, but it shows that arsenic may be introduced into the body by simple, gentle friction on an unbroken skin, and that the poisoned shirt theory was possible.

The administration of poison in the form of medicine is another method which has often been criminally employed. In France, the enema was at one time frequently made use of for introducing arsenic, corrosive sublimate, and opium into the system. The poisoner's aim, in such cases, was to attribute the fatal effects which followed to disease. Within recent years a curious case was tried at the Paris Court of Assizes, in which a lady was charged with attempting to poison her husband. It was known that the couple had lived unhappily together, and arrangements had been made for a divorce. One morning the husband complained of a severe headache, and his wife suggested a dose of antipyrine, which she gave him in some mineral water. He remarked to her at the time that the draught had a peculiar taste. Later in the day she administered sundry cups of coffee to him; but he grew rapidly worse and at night a doctor was summoned. He failed to diagnose the complaint, and called in other medical men, who were equally puzzled. One thing which they all noticed, was a peculiar dilation of the pupils of the patient's eyes.

A consultation was held the next day, and shortly afterwards one of the medical men received a note from the lady, in which she stated, that her husband "was black. He was dead, more dead than any man I ever saw."

The doctor at once went to see the patient, and found him in a state of collapse. He bled him twice and injected caffeine, but he still remained motionless. After a time it occurred to the doctor that the patient's symptoms resembled those of atropine poisoning, and, resorting to other measures, he eventually brought him round. Then he remembered, that the lady had previously asked him for some morphine for herself, and when he had refused it, she requested some atropine for her dog's eyes. He wrote her a prescription for a solution of atropine, containing ten per cent. of the drug, and took it to the chemist himself. On further inquiries it was proved that the lady had procured atropine upon various other occasions by copying the doctor's prescription and forging his signature.

At the trial, the medical evidence was very conflicting; but the concensus of opinion was in favour of the theory that atropine had been administered in small, repeated doses. The accused woman declared in her defence, that atropine had been put into the medicine for her husband in mistake by the chemist who had dispensed it. There was no evidence to support this theory, and she was found guilty and sentenced to five years' penal servitude.

A strange method, which said to have been employed by the Borgias, and was afterwards used in France, was a combination of arsenic with the secretions or products of decomposition of an animal to which it had been administered. The poison was prepared by cutting open a pig, and well sprinkling the carcase with arsenic or other poison. Then it was left to putrefy, after which the liquids that ran from the decaying mass were collected, and these formed the finished poison.

As science advances, opening up fresh fields for research and poisons of a still more deadly nature are revealed, so the chemist sets to work to discover methods for their certain detection, and thus renders the poisoners' fiendish work more difficult.

It is well to remember that even the most deadly poisons have their proper use, and in skilled hands prove valuable instruments in combating many diseases that afflict suffering humanity.

THE END